THE RED ABBEY CHRONICLES

MARESI

AMULET BOOKS
NEW YORK

1/17 Ingram $7.95

Cataloging-in-Publication Data has been applied for and may be obtained from the Library of Congress.

ISBN: 978-1-4197-2269-1

Text copyright © 2014 Maria Turtschaninoff
Translation copyright © 2016 A.A. Prime
Display type by Alyssa Nassner
Book design by Pamela Notarantonio
Maps by Sara Corbett

ABRAMS The Art of Books
115 West 18th Street, New York, NY 10011
abramsbooks.com

FOR ALEXANDRIA,
MY SISTER

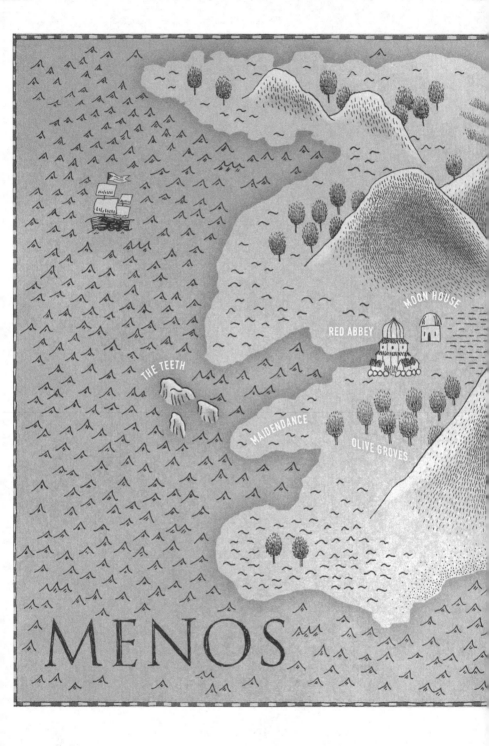

MOON HOUSE

RED ABBEY

THE TEETH

MAIDENDANCE

OLIVE GROVES

MENOS

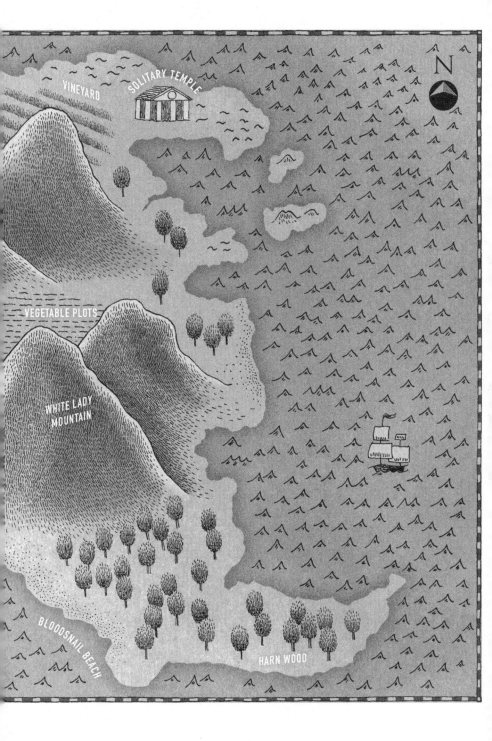

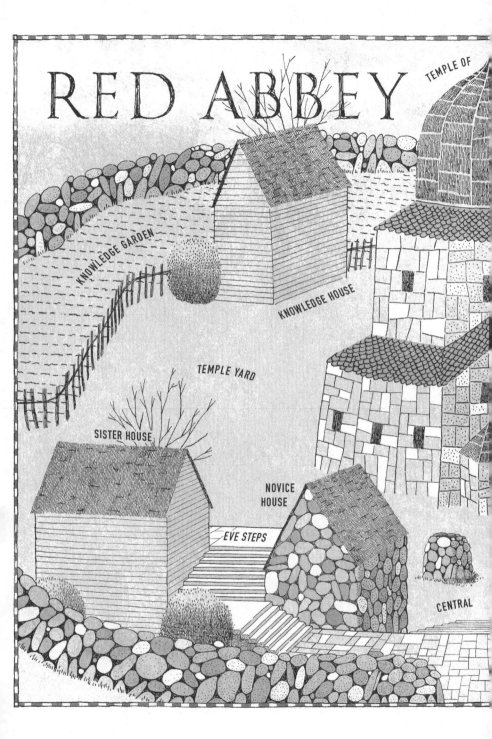

RED ABBEY

TEMPLE OF

KNOWLEDGE GARDEN

KNOWLEDGE HOUSE

TEMPLE YARD

SISTER HOUSE

NOVICE
HOUSE

EVE STEPS

CENTRAL

My name is Maresi Enresdaughter and I write this in the nineteenth year of the reign of our thirty-second Mother. In the four years since I came to the Red Abbey I have read nearly all the ancient scriptures about its history. Sister O says that this story of mine will become a new addition to the archives. It seems strange. I am only a novice, not an abbess, not a learned sister. But Sister O says it is important that I am the one who writes down what happened. I was there. Secondhand stories are not to be trusted.

I am no storyteller. Not yet. But by the time I am and can tell the story as it should be told, I will have forgotten. So I am recording my memories now, while they are still fresh and sharp in my mind. Not much time has passed, only one spring. I can still vividly recall certain things I would rather forget. The smell of blood. The sound of crunching bones. I do not want to bring it all up again. But I have to. It is difficult to write about death. But that is no excuse not to.

I am telling the story to make sure the Abbey never forgets. But also so that I can fully grasp what happened. Reading has always helped me to understand the world better. I hope the same applies to writing.

I am thinking about my words more than anything. Which ones will conjure up the right images without distorting or embellishing the truth? What is the weight of my words? I will do my best only to describe what is relevant to my story and leave out everything else, but Goddess forgive me if I do not always succeed in my task.

It is also difficult to know where a story begins and ends. I do not know where the ending is. It does not feel like it has come yet. But the beginning is easy. It all began when Jai came to the island.

I was harvesting mussels down on the beach on the spring morning when Jai arrived. When my basket was half full I sat down on a rock to rest for a moment. The sun had not climbed up over White Lady Mountain yet, the beach was in shade and my feet were cold from the seawater. The round pebbles beneath my feet rattled back and forth in rhythm with the motion of the sea. A red-billed koan bird hopped at the water's edge, also looking for mussels. The wading bird had just speared a shell with its long beak when a little boat appeared near the Teeth, the high, narrow rocks that protrude straight up out of the sea.

Fishing boats come by several times per moon, so I might have thought nothing of it had the ship not been arriving from such an unusual direction. The fishermen we trade with travel from the mainland in the North, or the rich fishing waters of the islands in the East. Their boats are small, white-painted vessels, nothing like this ship heading toward the island. The fishermen's sails are blue and the boats have a crew of two or three men.

The ones that come from the mainland bringing provisions, and sometimes new novices, are slow, round-bellied ships that often have a watchman to guard against pirates. When I came here in such a ship four years ago it was the first time I had ever seen the ocean.

I did not even know what the ship was called that I saw come sailing around the Teeth, heading straight for our harbor. I had only seen that kind of ship a handful of times. They come from far Western lands such as Emmel and Samitra, and other lands even farther away.

But even those ships usually come from the direction of the mainland, along the same route as the fishing boats. They sail along the coast and only venture out into this deep water at the last possible moment. Our island is very small and difficult to find if you do not follow the regular route. Sister Loeni says it is the First Mother who veils the island, but Sister O snorts and mutters something about incompetent sailors. I believe it is the island that hides itself. But this vessel still managed to find us somehow, despite coming around the Teeth almost directly from the West. The boat's sail and slender hull were gray. Hard to spot on a gray sea. It was a ship that did not want to announce its arrival.

When I could see that the ship was heading for our little harbor I jumped up and ran toward it over the cobbled beach. I am ashamed to say I forgot my basket and mussels. That is the type of thing Sister Loeni is always telling me off for. You are too impulsive, Maresi, she says. Look at Mother. Would she abandon her duties like that?

I cannot imagine she would. Then again I also cannot picture Mother with rolled-up trousers and seaweed between her toes, bent over a basket of mussels. She must have done it once, when she was a young novice like me. But I cannot imagine Mother as a little girl. It simply does not make sense.

Sister Veerk and Sister Nummel were ready to meet the ship on the pier, gazing out at the gray sails. They did not see me. I snuck closer quietly and carefully so the pier's creaking planks would not give me away. I wondered what stout Sister Nummel was doing there. She is in charge of the junior novices, and reedy Sister Veerk is the one who handles trade with fishermen.

"Is this what Mother foresaw?" asked Sister Nummel, shielding her eyes with her dimpled hand.

"Perhaps," answered Sister Veerk. She will never speculate if she is not sure.

"I certainly hope not. Her words in the trance were difficult to decipher but the message was clear." Sister Nummel adjusted her headscarf. "Danger. Great danger."

A plank creaked under my foot. The sisters turned around. Sister Nummel frowned.

"Maresi. What are you doing here? You are supposed to be working at Hearth House today."

"Yes." I dragged out my answer. "I was harvesting mussels, but then I saw the ship."

Sister Veerk pointed. "Look, they are hauling in the sails."

We watched in silence as the crew maneuvered the vessel into the harbor. It seemed odd how few people there were aboard. There was a bearded old man in a blue tunic at the capstan and I guessed he must be the captain. I could only see three other men, all with hard faces and stern expressions. The captain stepped off first and Sister Veerk went to speak with him. When I tried to sneak closer to hear what they were saying Sister Nummel took me firmly by the arm. Soon Sister Veerk came back and whispered something to Sister Nummel, who immediately started to pull me away from the pier.

Even though I went with Sister Nummel without protest, I could not curb my curiosity. I wanted to be the one who brought the news back to the other novices. Twisting and turning my head, I caught a glimpse of the captain helping someone up from inside the ship. A slight figure with a cascade of fair, tangled hair over slender shoulders. She wore a straight brown sleeveless chemise over a shirt that might have been white once. Her clothes were worn and, although at first I thought her chemise was made of thick silk, when she moved I could see that in fact it was stiff with dirt. I could not see her face, she was staring at the ground as though she had to study every step she took. As though she were afraid to trust the ground beneath her feet. I did not know it at the time, but this was Jai.

I did not understand why Sister Nummel had been so

anxious to get me away from the pier. Later that day Jai appeared in Novice House with the rest of us. Her long hair was still not clean, but it was combed and smooth and she was dressed like the rest of us in brown trousers, white shirt, and a white headscarf. If I had not seen her arrive, I would never have known she was any different from the rest of us.

Jai got the bed next to mine. New novices usually have to sleep in the junior novices' dormitory, but that is because most new arrivals are little girls. Jai was old enough to sleep with us older girls. I guessed that she was fourteen or fifteen, a year or two older than me.

The bed next to mine in the senior novices' dormitory was free because Joem had just moved into Hearth House to become novice to Sister Ers. Her novices are the only ones who do not sleep in Novice House. They have to keep the Hearth fire burning, the fire that must never go out, and they have to make offerings to Havva at all the right times. Joem thinks she is special because she gets to be a servant to the Hearth, with the soot mark on both cheeks as an insignia. She is sure she will succeed Sister Ers as Mistress of the Hearth, and get her marks permanently tattooed on. But Sister Ers is young, so if that's what Joem wants she will have to wait a long time. I know Joem believes that everybody envies her. When I first came to the island I could not imagine anything better than living in Hearth House, always surrounded by food. My stomach could not forget the hunger winter we had endured back home. But I soon changed my mind when I saw how strict Sister Ers was, never allowing her novices extra portions. Imagine constantly touching food, smelling food, working with food, but not being allowed to eat it!

Besides, Joem talked in her sleep. I did not miss her.

Jai sat on her bed and all the novices, younger and older, flocked around her as we always do when there is a new arrival. The little girls admired the long blond hair flowing out of her linen headscarf. Our headscarves protect us from the strong sun, but under them our hair must never be bound. We never cut our hair either. Our hair holds our strength, Sister O says.

The older girls quizzed her about where she came from, how long she had traveled, whether she had known anything about the Abbey before. Jai sat completely still. Her complexion was fairer than most, but I could tell that she was unusually pale. The skin under her eyes was thin and dark, nearly purple. Like violets in spring. She did not say a thing or answer a single question, she just looked around.

I got up from my bed. "That's enough. You have all got duties to be getting on with. Off you go."

They all did as they were told. It is funny to think that when I first came I was always making mistakes and no one would ever have done what I said. Now I was one of the oldest in Novice House who still did not answer to a specific house or sister. I was one of the longest-serving novices. The only one who had been around longer than me and still did not have a sister of her own was Ennike.

I showed Jai her cupboard and the clean clothes stacked inside, I told her where the outhouse was and helped her put new linen on her bed. She followed everything I did closely, but still said nothing.

"You do not need to do any duties today," I said, turning in the corners of her bedcover. "Later you will have to come to the Temple of the Rose for evening thanks, but do not worry, I will show you everything you need to know." I stood up straight. "Now it is nearly supper time. I will show you the way to Hearth House."

Jai still had not said a word.

"Do you understand what I am saying?" I asked softly. Maybe she came from such a faraway land that she did not even speak the coast languages. I did not when I first came. Up in the North, in lands like Rovas, Urundien, and Lavora, we speak a different language than they do down here by the sea. The coast languages are quite similar. People who speak them can understand one another, even though the pronunciation and certain words differ. Sister O says that the amount of mutual trade that goes on between the lands has ensured that their languages keep a close relationship. My first year at the Abbey was difficult before I learned the language.

Jai nodded. Then suddenly she opened her mouth to speak.

"Is it true there are no menfolk here?" Her voice was unexpectedly husky and her accent was one I had never heard before.

I shook my head. "Never. Men are not allowed on the island. The fishermen we trade with do not set foot on the land, Sister Veerk buys the catch from the pier. We have male animals of course. One quite savage rooster, some billy goats. But no men."

"How do you get by? Who takes care of the animals and works the earth and protects you?"

I led her to the tall, narrow door of the dormitory. There are so many doors here, each different from the last. They shut out, they lock in, they protect, hide, veil, conceal. They look at me with their bright iron fittings, stare with large wooden knots, glare with carved patterns. I counted that on any given day I pass by at least twenty doors.

Back home we had two. The cottage door and the outhouse door. Both were made of wooden planks hung on leather hinges that Father had made. At night Father would bar the cottage door from the inside with a big beam. The outhouse could be closed from the inside with a latch, and my brother Akios would flick it up from the outside with a splinter of wood while my sister Náraes would scream at him to leave us alone.

I led Jai through the corridor of Novice House. "We do not grow any grain ourselves, the island is too rocky. We buy what we need from the mainland. But we have some vegetable plots and olive groves and the sisters grow vines for wine at the Solitary Temple. We only drink it a few times a year at festivals and rituals."

We came out into the warm evening sun and I pulled my headscarf down over my eyes. Sister Loeni does not approve when I do that, she says it is unbecoming, but I do not like having the sun in my eyes.

"We do not need protection. Few sail this far out. Did you not see how steep the mountain up to the Abbey is, and the high wall surrounding it? There are only two entrances in the outer wall. The one you came through can be closed with a heavy door and bolted. The other one is called the goat door and it goes up toward the mountain." I pointed. "It leads to a little path we follow when we take the goats out to graze, and from there it goes to the Solitary Temple and White Lady, and our vegetable plots. It is very difficult to find the door from the mountainside if you do not already know where it is. And it has been a long time since pirates attacked the Abbey. It happened when the First Sisters came, which is why they built the outer wall, but it has not happened since. The Abbey is the only settlement on the

14

island. There is no one we need to protect ourselves from." I made the sign of the circle on my left palm with my right index finger to ward off bad luck. "We are all servants of the First Mother. She protects us if we are in need."

The central courtyard was empty. Everybody must have already gone to Hearth House. That is always the way once word gets around that we have fresh fish. Before I came here I had only eaten dried fish a few times and it barely tasted of anything. But Sister Ers uses herbs and rare spices in all the cooking at Hearth House. The first time I put a spoonful of stew in my mouth the taste was so unfamiliar that I nearly spat it out again. The only thing that stopped me was the disapproval in the sisters' watchful eyes, which was lucky. If I had spat it out I would have accidentally exposed my ignorance to everyone. I felt uneducated and awkward enough as it was. Later I came to learn the names of all the unusual flavors. Cinnamon from the East, goosefoot from the Northern lands, yellow iruk and wild oregano from our own mountain slopes.

I looked at Jai. She must have felt just as awkward as I did when I came to the island. I reached out my hand to give her an encouraging pat on the arm, but she flinched as if I were about to hit her. She froze and hid her face in her hands. Her cheeks went even paler than before.

"Do not be scared," I said gently. "I only want to show you the houses. See, that is Body's Spring. You will learn about that tomorrow. Those steps lead up to the Temple Yard and Knowledge House, Sister House and the Temple of the Rose. They are called Eve Steps because they lead westward."

I saw Jai peek through her fingers so I carried on talking. "We call that long, narrow staircase Moon Steps. There are two hundred and seventy steps! I counted them myself. They lead up to the Moon Yard and Moon House. Mother's chamber is up there. Have you met Mother yet?"

Jai lowered her hands and nodded. I knew she had met Mother, all girls do as soon as they arrive. That was not why I asked her. I wanted to get her to relax.

"We do not have reason to go up there very often. Now I will take you up Dawn Steps. They lead up to Hearth House and the storehouse. Come."

I was wary of taking her by the hand to lead her, so I

settled for walking in front and hoping she followed. She did follow, a few steps behind. I carried on babbling to keep her calm, like I do with the chickens when I collect their eggs. Sister Mareane laughs at me when I do that, but she lets me be. Sister Loeni, on the other hand, is always trying to get me to be quiet. But Sister Mareane knows that a gentle voice can soothe easily frightened animals.

"Wait until you see how well we eat here! The first time someone told me we get meat or fish for supper every day I laughed in her face. I thought she was joking. Eating meat every day! But it is no joke. It is usually fish or meat from our own goats. Some novices think there is too much goat meat, but not I—Sister Ers makes so many different tasty things with goat. Goat sausages and goat steak and goat stew and dried goat meat. And goat's milk of course. It is made into all sorts of cheeses. We keep chickens mainly for eggs, but sometimes a bird will find its way into one of Sister Ers's stews. Sister Ers is the tattooed sister in charge of Hearth House. All the sisters have their own responsibilities, as you will see for yourself soon enough." We puffed and panted our way up the last steps. When we came to the courtyard in front of Hearth House I could smell white fish and cooked egg. My stomach rumbled. However much I eat, I always seem to be hungry. It has been that way ever since the hunger winter.

"We all eat the same thing," I said, approaching the Hearth House door. "From the youngest novice to the sisters and Mother herself. Only the sisters in the Solitary Temple eat differently. Novices eat first, then the sisters. The same goes with washing, as you will see in the morning."

I opened the Hearth House door, which, as always, smelled like bread. When I first came here I could not resist the temptation to lick the hazel-brown wood to see if it tasted like bread too. Sister O scolded me all moon for my stupidity. Now I am older and I know better. But the door still smells like bread.

Jai was completely silent again. I was definitely talking too much. Sister Loeni would say so anyway. But Jai did not seem so tense and flighty anymore. She sat next to me and let Joem serve her a portion of white fish and cooked egg with stewed korr-root from the southern slopes of the island. I was glad to have korr-root and not cabbage. There is often a great deal of cabbage in our diet.

When we had finished eating I leaned back on the bench and patted my round belly.

"No one back home would believe me if I told them how well we eat here."

It is painful to think about my family having less to eat than we do at the Abbey. Maybe they go hungry sometimes. My home is so far away that I do not know what their winter was like this year, how the harvest went, or whether they have food on the table. I can only hope that with one less mouth to feed they have more left for the others. I could write them a letter but no one back home can read, and I do not even know how I would get a letter to our little farm, all the way up in the northernmost part of the great valley of Rovas.

I shook away my sorrow and smiled encouragingly at Jai.

"Do not think about the past. You are with us now, and it is not nearly as strict as you might have heard rumored. After supper our time is our own."

Around us, novices moved under the watchful eyes of Sister Ers, carrying their cups and plates to the scullery. Sister Ers's novices wiped the long table clean so it would be presentable for the sisters when it was their turn to eat. I took my plate and cup, Jai did the same and we stood in the line to the scullery.

"Lots of novices like to go down to the beach in the evening to swim or collect shells," I said. "Others wander up into the mountains to pick flowers and enjoy the view. Many do their reading assignments from Sister O or Sister Nummel, others chat or play games."

We put our plates in a tub of cold water. We were the last to leave the scullery and come back out into the evening sun. Bleats were coming from the goat house. It was nearly milking time. Several sisters were on their way up Dawn Steps to supper, deep in conversation. I would have to hurry to get to Sister O's room before she left.

"You can find your way back to Novice House, can't you? You can do whatever you like until it is time for evening thanks in the Temple of the Rose."

"Can I come with you?"

Jai's husky voice surprised me again. She stood with her hands clasped in front of her and eyes cast down at the ground. My heart sank. I did not want to take Jai with me. My evening activity was my own. I had never shared it with anybody.

"You'd only be bored," I said hesitantly. "You see, I . . ."

She stood completely still. Her hands gripped each other so hard her knuckles went white. She did not look me in the eye. I could not bring myself to deny a little company to a lonely girl on her first night in a new place.

"Of course you can join me if you want." She looked up at once and I smiled at her. "Come, we had better hurry!"

I ran down Dawn Steps, bumping into several sisters and mumbling apologies to them as I went. Sister Loeni got such a shove that her headscarf half fell off. She screwed up her face in that way that makes even her prominent chin wrinkle.

"Maresi! Look where you are going! If Mother ever . . ." Her chiding words faded into the distance as I ran across the central courtyard's uneven paving stones and rushed up Eve Steps with Jai close behind.

The Temple Yard has buildings on three of its sides and below the fourth side is the roof of Novice House. To the west, toward the wall, is Sister House. To the east, toward the mountainside, is the beautiful Temple of the Rose, and to the north is the Abbey's oldest building, Knowledge House. Behind Knowledge House is the Knowledge Yard, with its solitary lemon tree, and along one side of the courtyard is Knowledge Garden, protected from the sea winds by a low wall.

I ran up to Sister House, opened the door, and ran down the corridor to Sister O's room. I could hear Jai's steps behind me.

You have to knock on Sister O's door using a little brass knocker designed for the purpose. It is in the shape of a snake biting its own tail. When I asked Sister O about the snake she smiled her crooked little smile and said it was her guardian. I have learned not to ask her too many questions at once. But I resolved that one day I would find out exactly what she meant by that.

I knocked and Sister O called "Come in," sternly, as always. I opened the heavy oak door. Sister O was sitting at a large desk under the western window, bent over piles of parchments and books. Her fingers were flecked with black ink and she wore linen cloth on her arms so as not to get it on her shirt.

Usually when she sees that it is me she just raises her eyebrows and points at the key hanging on its hook under the wall-mounted candleholder. But when she saw Jai standing behind me she put down her quill and sat up straight.

"Who is this?" she asked with her characteristic abruptness, and I sensed Jai flinch. I stepped out of the way so they could see each other.

"This is Jai, she arrived today. I am going to show her the treasure chamber."

I blushed. I try not to use that term around anyone else. It is only a childish name I gave the room when I first saw what was in there. I know that the key does not open the way to some kind of treasure trove. But for me it is the best place on the whole island.

Sister O had already gone back to work. She motioned toward the key and turned a page of the book in front of her. I think more often than not she forgets to go to supper.

I lifted down the key. It is as long as my hand and ornately decorated. I always hold it in the same way, with a firm grip on its elegant handle. I waved Jai out and shut the door quietly behind me. Then I grinned. I could not help it. I get the same feeling of jittery excitement every time.

The treasure chamber is in Knowledge House, past our classrooms, at the far end of the long, echoing stone corridor. In the evenings the house is empty and the doors to the classrooms are closed. Ennike asked me once how I dare go there alone after sundown when the house is empty and still. It had never occurred to me to be scared. I did not know what there would be to fear.

This was the first time I had been there in the evening with somebody else, and it bothered me. We rarely get to be alone at the Abbey. My time in the treasure chamber was the only time all day that was totally and utterly my own. But I was trying to be kind to Jai. She probably will not even want to stay once she has seen it, I thought, maybe she will find an Abbey cat to play with or another novice to talk to. Though she did not exactly seem talkative.

Like all the rooms in Knowledge House, the treasure chamber has double doors that are tall and narrow. They are made of a reddish-brown wood sanded and polished to a shine. Sister O takes care of them herself. She is there several times per moon with a ladder, a jar of beeswax, and a big, soft rag, rubbing and polishing. It certainly is not one of her official duties, as I understood when I heard Sister Loeni tut in that disapproving way of hers. But I understand why Sister O does it. Some doors shut you out, some keep secrets, and others keep something dangerous locked in. These doors form a comforting, protective barrier around the treasure chamber. I would happily help Sister O polish their beautiful grain. One day I will ask her.

I put the key in the lock and the honey-scented doors swung open without a sound.

Jai gasped.

The treasure chamber is a long, narrow room. Both the long walls are covered with shelves from floor to ceiling. On the short wall at the far end there is a high, narrow window that lets the evening sun stream in. It is the highest window I have ever seen, and it has twenty-one panes of glass. The sunlight falls softly over the spines of all the thousands of books on the shelves, and I usually simply stand there a moment, breathing in the scent of dust and parchments and bliss. It is the best part of the day. It makes everything worth it: living here, away from my family, far from our lush valley between the towering hills. Lying in bed night after night with a pining in my heart. Eating porridge all those gray winter mornings. Being scolded by the sisters and told off by the older novices before I knew how things were done, what to do and what not to do. Barely understanding people speaking around me for a whole year. All of that and much more is worth it just to stand there filled with anticipation and a sort of yearning, but a good one. A yearning that makes my cheeks flush and my heartbeat quicken.

Jai walked up to one of the shelves. She stroked the spines of the books reverently with the tips of her fingers and then turned to me.

"I did not know so many books existed in the whole world!"

"Neither did I before I came here. Can you read?"

Jai nodded. "My mother taught me." She tilted her head back and ran her eyes all the way up to the top of the shelves. "So many . . ." she repeated in awe.

"You can read any book you want. Although those scrolls at the top are old and fragile so you can only touch them under Sister O's supervision."

I could not contain myself any longer. Jai could take care of herself. I went to pick out the book I had been reading the night before, and another, and another. I carried them to one of the desks by the window where I can read in the light that falls over my shoulder. There are oil lamps around the room but I am not allowed to light them. It does not matter, though, because the window catches the dusky sunlight long into the evening, and, besides, I have sharp young eyes. I can read even when it grows dark. Once I got so lost in my reading that I did not know evening thanks had started and only realized how late it was when I saw

Sister O looking at me from the doorway. I did not know how long she had been standing there and I jumped up, gushing apologies like a fountain, and ran around putting all the books back, my heart fluttering like a startled bird. Sister O watched me in silence, which frightened me more than her usual curt words. But when I came closer I saw that her thin lips were drawn up in a little smile and her eyes were warm. She stroked my hair. It was the first time anyone had done that since I had left my own mother. A lump in my throat prevented me from speaking. She tucked a stray lock of my brown hair back behind my ear and gave me a soft pat on the cheek. Then we left together, I locked the doors behind us and handed her the key. She led me out of Knowledge House to the Temple of the Rose, where she helped me sneak in unnoticed and I managed to avoid a scolding. That time at least.

After that Sister O was just as strict with me as before, but I was not so afraid of her. One time when I came to her chamber she was so deeply absorbed in her reading that she did not even notice I was there. Her headscarf was completely crooked and she scratched her gray hair absentmindedly with one hand while slowly turning the pages of her book with the other. And then I knew. She was just like me.

I opened the book ravenously and began reading. The room was completely silent. Outside I could hear the sea's eternal whisper and the calls of a seabird. I read for a long time. Only when I had finished the first book and picked up a second did I remember about Jai. I looked up.

She was sitting in a patch of sun on the floor with a book open on her lap. The book was so big that her legs were hidden beneath it. The evening sun drifted slowly across the floor, and when eventually it fell away from the pages of the book she shuffled laboriously back into the light without getting up. Her neck remained softly tilted downward. When it was time to put the books away and go to evening thanks, I had to tell her several times before she heard me.

After that I was never alone in the treasure chamber in the evenings. I soon got used to Jai's presence because she was as quiet as a mouse and always did as I asked. It was not long before it felt as though we had always been there together.

Jai's first morning at the Abbey was a sunny one. We usually have beautiful weather in spring. In autumn the First Mother combs her hair and storms lash at the island. At those times we hardly dare go outside for fear of being dashed against the mountainsides. But that morning the warmth was returning. Our island, Menos, had not yet put on its cloak of spring flowers but the pastures were lush and green, much to the delight of the goats.

When we had all risen, made our beds, and lined up, I opened the dormitory door. Sister Nummel made sure we were all present before leading us out to the central courtyard. It was still so early and chilly that the stones were dark with dew. Sister Nummel led us through the sun greeting. We always do the sun greeting as the sun rises up over the sea in the East, granting us her warmth and life. Before I came here I did not know that the sun was so important and that no life could exist without her. I am glad I know now, and I was always glad to greet her together with the other novices. I longed for the day when I could welcome the sun with the other sisters up in the Temple Yard. You can see the sunrise and sunset better from up there than down in the central courtyard.

I showed Jai how to do the movements and whispered to her what they meant. We are not usually allowed to talk during the sun greeting but Sister Nummel made an exception because Jai was new. I looked around to see whether anybody noticed that this time I was the one who was allowed to break the rule, instead of the one everyone else could correct. Joem gave me a look and turned up her nose. She never lets on that she is impressed with anyone.

When we were done Sister Nummel led us through the central courtyard and up to Body's Spring, where Sister Kotke was waiting for us. She is in charge of Body's Spring. The vapor rising from the water means her skin is always slightly puckered and makes her clothes damp so they cling to her round body like eel skin. The stone door is too heavy for one woman, so the sisters opened it together.

I helped Jai get undressed. She hesitated until she saw all the other novices doing the same. When I got her shirt off I understood why. She had ugly scars all over her back, as if she had been beaten with a whip or a cane. She is not the only one.

There are many reasons why a girl might come to this island. Sometimes poor families from the coast lands send a daughter here because they cannot provide for her. Sometimes a family notices that their daughter has a sharp and inquiring mind and want to give her the best education a woman can get. Sometimes sick or disabled girls come here because they know the sisters can give them the best possible care. Like Ydda, who was born shorter than most and whose family could not look after her. When she was sent here, her twin sister Ranna refused to be separated from her and so followed along.

Sometimes a rich man invests in his daughter by sending her to the Abbey and paying for her education. Maybe he does not think she can get a husband because she is ugly or for some other reason. A woman who has spent her childhood at the Abbey can always find a place in the world.

Take Joem, for example. Her father sent her here because he wanted her to become an expert cook so that it would be easier for him to marry her off. Joem has four sisters who are more beautiful than her and married long ago. I wonder if this was why she seemed so bitter at times.

Sometimes girls come here as runaways, mainly from Urundien and the surrounding states, or one of the numerous Western lands. Girls who show a thirst for knowledge in cultures where women are not allowed to know or say anything. In these lands rumor of the Abbey's existence lives in women's songs and forbidden folk tales told only in whispers, away from enemy ears. Nobody talks openly about our island, but most people have heard of it anyway. Ennike is one of those runaway girls, as is Heo, the little black-haired Akkade girl from Namar, the walled city on the border between Urundien and the Akkades' land. They have marks on their bodies like Jai's. I had suspected that Jai had gone through something similar in her past, but now I knew for sure.

Jai followed me down the smooth marble steps into the warm bathing pool. The water comes from a hot underground spring. We walked hand in hand through the pool and to the steps at the other end. Lots of the novices can swim, but not I. Jai did not seem scared of the water but she moved through it anxiously. Almost as though she were trying to shield herself from it as it swirled around her.

From the hot bath we went down to the cold one, and my word is it cold! Sometimes I wish we did it the other way around and warmed up in the hot bath last, but on a hot summer day it does feel wonderful to cool off before getting dressed again.

After we had washed, Sister Nummel led us out through the stone doors to let the sisters have their turn. They bathe after us because they have morning rituals to perform first. Then it was time for breakfast in Hearth House. When Jai sat next to me I understood that she had decided to become my shadow. That is what we usually say when a new novice latches onto someone who has been around longer. She follows her like a shadow until she finds her place. It was the first time I had had one and it was not without a certain pride. I stretched and smiled at Ennike, who was sitting opposite us. I used to be her shadow. She reminds me of my sister Náraes because she has the same curly hair and warm brown eyes. It took several weeks before I was brave enough to let her out of my sight. She did not get annoyed with me even once. I made up my mind to be just as patient and generous toward Jai.

That morning we finally got fresh bread again. Sister Ers and her novices had celebrated Havva's festival the day before, and now the oven was cleaned and blessed and we could bake again. After several moons of nothing but porridge it was a feast to sink my teeth into salty bread warm from the oven. I grinned at Ennike, my mouth full of bread, and she laughed.

"No one loves spring bread quite as much as you, Maresi!"

"Yup, and there is only one thing I love more than spring bread." We looked at each other, giggled and shouted, "Nadum bread!" in one voice.

It is easy to laugh with Ennike. It is one of the things I like about her.

Jai sat and picked at her food. She had eaten some bread but left the pickled onion and smoked fish. I pointed at her plate.

"Just wait until summer! Then we get a cooked egg with the bread and a thick wedge of goat's cheese. And once the Spring Star has gone back into slumber, we get honey!"

"You should see Maresi at autumn breakfasts," said Ennike. "They bake nutty, seedy nadum bread in the kitchen and Maresi waits outside the Hearth House door before anyone else, sniffing like a hungry dog! We get cheese and bright-red nirnberry sauce in autumn too."

"They make the sauce with mint and honey. Sister Ers always says it is good enough to offer to the First Mother herself." I licked my lips at the thought.

Ennike looked curiously at Jai. "What kind of food did you get back home?"

Jai closed up like a mussel, hunched inward with a far-off look in her eyes. I shook my head at Ennike and quickly changed the subject to distract Jai from Ennike's question.

"If it were not for autumn breakfasts I do not think I could put up with the never-ending winter porridge," I said. "Porridge, porridge, porridge, day in day out. You know what I dream about all winter long?"

Jai did not answer but Ennike smiled and nodded. "Moon Dance! After the dance we have a huge feast up in the Moon Yard."

"Then we get koan egg in spicy sauce. The koan bird

is the symbol of our Abbey and we only eat its egg after Moon Dance. Sister Ers serves it with delicious crispy meat pies and sesame biscuits sprinkled with cinnamon." I had to swallow. The thought of all that tasty food was making my mouth water. Ennike took a sip from her cup.

"And we get to drink something other than just water. Strong mead and sweetened wine!"

"The steps down to Novice House feel very long when your belly is full of food!"

We laughed. Ennike and I, that is, not Jai, but she seemed to have opened up a little. I was pleased that I could help her relax. I got up from the table.

"Come on. It is lesson time."

We offered the last of our bread to the Hearth, walked down Dawn Steps, across the central courtyard, and up Eve Steps to Knowledge House. Knowledge House is the oldest structure on the island. Sister O taught us that it was the first and probably the most important building that the First Sisters built after they sailed here in the ship *Naondel*.

It is my job to stand by the cracked wooden door to the junior novices' classroom, making sure they all sit still until the sister arrives to take their lesson. Jai followed Ennike to our classroom while I ushered in the late girls, the last of whom is always Heo. That morning I found her sitting under the lemon tree out in the Knowledge Yard, stroking a gray Abbey cat that lay on its side purring. As I approached she looked up at me, and it occurred to me that her slanting eyes always look as if they are laughing.

"Can't I take him with me to class, Maresi?"

"You know you can't. Hurry up, Heo. Sister Nummel is coming soon and you do not want a scolding, now do you?"

"You get plenty of scoldings," said Heo as she stood up and put her little hand in mine. "I want to be like you."

I kissed her white headscarf. "Choose my good points and not my bad."

Hand in hand we hurried to the junior novice classroom and Heo just managed to sit down before Sister Nummel came sailing in, rotund and cheerful. She would never give Heo a scolding, and Heo knows that well enough.

Once the junior novices' class had started I ran to my own. I am the only one who is allowed to come late to the lesson. The door to the senior novices' classroom is made of old, cracked wood, similar to the junior novices' door but darker. I always close it very carefully behind me, afraid that if I slammed it the cracks would give way and the whole door would collapse.

I slipped into my spot on the worn wooden bench where we all sit along a large table. Sister O conducts the class from the front of the room. Only the oldest novices who are soon to become sisters do not come to lessons. They learn about their duties instead.

I love our lessons. We get to learn about history; mathematics; the First Mother; how the world works; about the moon, sun, and stars, and much more besides. The junior novices have to learn to read and write, if they cannot already, and lots of other things.

That day we were continuing our study of the history of the island.

"Do you remember how the First Sisters came here?" asked Sister O. I stood up at once, and she gave me a nod.

"Maresi?"

"The First Sisters decided to flee from a land where a wicked man had taken all the power and treated his people very badly," I answered. I had just read about it in a book in the treasure chamber. "He would not let anybody else have knowledge. The First Sisters refused to be his slaves so they stole as much knowledge as they could and sailed here in the ship *Naondel*."

Sister O nodded. "Their voyage was long and arduous. They came from the land far East, so far away that we no longer remember its name. Nobody has come to the Abbey from the Eastern lands since the First Sisters. It was a miracle that the boat did not smash on the rocks when a great storm heaved *Naondel* onto our island. Instead, the place where the ship landed marked the spot where the First Sisters were to build Knowledge House."

Ennike got up. "But how is that possible, Sister O?" She pointed out of the window. "Knowledge House is so high up the mountain. Not even the strongest autumn storms could throw a ship all the way up here."

Sister O nodded. "Indeed. But so it is written in the oldest texts. Perhaps the storms were worse then. Or perhaps the text should be interpreted in a different way."

I saw that Jai was listening intently. She sat leaning forward, her eyes transfixed on Sister O.

"Knowledge House conceals all the power the First Sisters brought with them," I recited from memory. "Sister O, why do they talk about power and not knowledge?"

"Because knowledge is power," said Dori.

Dori is Sister Mareane's novice and helps out with the animals. She is a few years older than me, but so absentminded and dreamy that she often seems younger. Dori is of the bird folk, and when she came to the island she brought one of their sacred birds with her. It is as big as a dove, with red and blue feathers, but the blue ones change color according to the light: sometimes green, sometimes black, sometimes golden. It usually sits on her shoulder, pecking and pulling at her black hair and jutting ears. It does not have a name, only Bird, and it seems to understand Dori when she speaks to it.

Sister O smiled at Dori and it was one of those rare moments when a smile softens her thin lips and dark eyes. "That is right, Dori. Knowledge is power. That is why it is so important that novices come here and take the knowledge back out into the world once we have taught them all we can, especially Sister Nar's novices, because they can share their knowledge of herbs and medicines all over the world."

"But other knowledge is important too," I interjected. I wanted to impress Sister O with how much I knew, even though I am younger than Dori. "Arithmetic and astronomy and history and . . . and . . ."

I could not come up with anything else.

"Cleanliness," Joem filled in. "Farming. How to feed many on little. To help prevent starvation."

"Animal care!" said Dori enthusiastically.

"Architecture," added Ennike. "How to build bridges, calculate durability, erect large buildings."

I was disappointed. I had wanted to come up with all of that myself.

"That is absolutely right," said Sister O seriously. "Any knowledge you can bring back to your homelands is important."

"But surely it is important that some novices stay here?

To keep the knowledge alive and pass it on to the new novices?" I asked.

"Yes," said Sister O. She looked at me with a solemn expression. "But our Abbey must not be used as an excuse to hide away from the world."

I did not entirely understand what she meant, but asked no more questions. All I knew was that on the island, with its warm sun, cool wind, and fragrant hillsides, amongst goats and bees and sisters and novices, I was home.

ꟃ

During the break Ennike and I went to our favorite place under the lemon tree. Jai came with us. We ate our bread, drank cold spring water, and gazed over the wall out to the silvery-blue sea, which shone so brightly it hurt our eyes. The air was filled with the sharp, sweet fragrance of the herbs and flowers Sister Nar grows in Knowledge Garden. Birds hovered on the breeze above us, sometimes alone, sometimes in flocks of gleaming white wings. A black cat with gray paws sat on the low garden wall grooming itself.

Ennike leaned back against the trunk of the lemon tree and stretched her legs.

"I hope I get called to a house or a sister soon. I cannot take Sister O's lessons anymore."

"But they are fascinating! We learn something new every day!" I gaped at her and she smiled.

"You can soak up knowledge like a sponge for days on end, Maresi. But I need to start doing something. Just think, if Mother called me as a servant to the Moon! That would be such an honor."

"You are the oldest novice on the island without a house. Of course she will choose you." I lay on my back and looked up at the tree's foliage. Small white flowers shone here and there amongst the dark leaves. The black cat jumped down from the wall and strutted toward us. Jai stretched out a cautious hand, and the cat rubbed its head against it and started to purr. Then suddenly Jai tensed up. I sat up and followed her gaze.

A little white boat with a blue sail was making its way into the harbor below.

"A fishing boat," I said softly, "coming to sell its catch.

Look, there is Sister Veerk and her novice Luan. They handle trade. Now they are going out on the pier, see? They will fill their baskets with fresh fish and then pay with copper coins or beeswax candles or maybe some healing ointment prepared by Sister Nar. She is the one who takes care of us when we are sick. She knows everything about healing and herbs. The fishermen usually tell us what they need so Sister Veerk can have it ready next time they come."

Jai still could not relax, so Ennike and I exchanged glances and got up.

"Lessons start again soon. Come on."

Jai soon got used to the Abbey's ways. I only had to show her something once and she remembered it. She took her dishes to the scullery when she had finished eating, she offered her bread to Havva, she took her clothes to Body's Spring for washing and she read the texts Sister O gave her every evening. She learned the movements of the sun greeting and the songs of thanks and praise within a few days. In the evenings she would come with me straight to Knowledge House and sit reading until sundown. She did not leave my side. The sisters noticed and did not separate us when they shared out duties, so Jai came with me to herd the goats up the mountain, harvest mussels on the beach, make the year's first batch of cheese, fetch water from the well, sweep the courtyards, and clean Novice House.

It soon became clear that Jai had not done much physical labor before. She was weak and could only carry half a bucket of water, but she never complained. She hardly ever spoke at all.

She had intense dreams at night and often woke me up with her anxious tossing and turning. I heard her mumble things I could not quite make out. She kept repeating one name: Unai. I did not know if that was a woman's or a man's name, but it must have been somebody very important because Jai dreamt about Unai every night. Lots of us sleep in the same dormitory, and I was not the only one who heard Jai's dreams.

Over the next few weeks spring came in full bloom. It started getting warmer and the sisters began talking about Moon Dance and all the other rituals of spring. Soon the mountains were draped in white and blue spring flowers and the air was alive with the hum of flies and bees. Dori strolled around singing along with the birds. She can mimic any bird perfectly.

One evening, half a moon after Jai's arrival, we were sitting together in our dormitory getting ready for bed. The older girls brushed the younger girls' hair, and I helped Ennike untangle her curls, which are always windswept and knotted by the end of the day.

She was sitting with her head back and her eyes shut. "My sister used to do this when I was little," she murmured. "I do not remember much about her other than the feel of her hands in my hair."

Heo sat by my feet and played with a kitten with fur as black as her own hair. The cat pounced on her fingers with its sharp teeth and claws, but Heo did not mind getting scratched.

"I don't have any sisters," she said. "Do you, Maresi?"

I nodded, brushing Ennike's hair until it shone. "One brother and two sisters. One of my sisters is older than me and my brother is your age, Heo. My big sister Náraes never had time to brush my hair. She helped our mother with the farm and I took care of the little ones." I swallowed. It was still difficult for me to talk about Anner. "My youngest sister—"

Jai was mending a hole in her trousers with a needle and thread. As I braced myself to carry on talking I saw that her sewing had fallen onto her lap and her cheeks had gone as white as the snow up on White Lady's peak. Just then Heo interrupted me.

"Jai, who is Unai? I have heard you say the name at night."

"Heo!" I said sharply, and she looked up at me with her big brown eyes, taken aback by my tone. At the same moment Jai let out a high-pitched, whimpering cry. It was a terrible sound. She raised her hands and smacked herself in the face, over and over again until I leapt forward and grabbed hold of her hands. But I could not stop her wailing. I turned to Ennike without letting go.

"Get Sister Nummel!"

Ennike rushed out of the room as the other novices moved out of the way. Heo had curled up into a little ball between the beds and was silent. Before long Sister Nummel came rushing in and together we led Jai to Sister Nummel's bed. Jai did not protest, but we had to hold her hands to stop her trying to slap or scratch at herself. Ennike ran to fetch Sister Nar, who swiftly turned up with a tincture she made Jai drink. It afforded her a little calm and soon she lay subdued on Sister Nummel's bed.

The sisters shooed me and Ennike away, and we had a hard time trying to get the agitated junior novices into bed. When the dorms were finally quiet, Ennike and I went out to get a breath of fresh air and calm down.

The indigo sky, dotted with stars, arched over the central courtyard. Everything was quiet but for the sea's gentle hush beyond the wall. Ennike took a deep breath.

"She has gone through even worse things than I have. I was often beaten by my father and grandfather, but she has had worse than beatings."

I tried to understand what it would be like to be hit by your own father. I thought about my skinny little papa, who gave up his own portions to us children in that never-ending winter. I thought about how he had gathered together all the stories he could about the Abbey, where it was and how to get there. How he wept when he realized that living in the Abbey would be the best thing for me. How he would not let go of my hand as I sat in the cart that was to take me away from our home, from our village, from our land, to the far-off southern coast.

"She does not know how to feel safe." As I said it I knew it was true. "We will have to teach her how."

We are mostly self-sufficient at the Abbey. We harvest mussels, birds' eggs, berries and fruits from mountain and sea. We have goats for milk and cheese and meat, and we grow vegetables in one of the valleys between the Abbey and the Solitary Temple. There are also some olive trees and vineyards by the Solitary Temple, and we get honey from Sister Mareane's beehives.

But we do have to buy grains, fish, salt, and spices, as well as fabric for clothes and incense for our censers. All these things require silver, but the Abbey has more than enough of that, thanks to the bloodsnail.

The bloodsnail is the only way to dye fabric truly crimson. You can get plenty of different reddish shades with various plants, but none of them give the same deep, brilliant red color as the bloodsnail. I think the color is beautiful, of course, but it still amazes me how sought after it is in all the known lands and how high a price it commands. Bloodsnail red dyes the garments of kings and fabrics of the rich. Only those with a heavy purse can afford the color. The bloodsnail is what gave the Red Abbey its name, or so I thought, but when I said so to Sister O she replied that there were probably several reasons. It is also about the sacred lifeblood and things I did not entirely understand yet.

When Mother was a girl, bloodsnail red did not fetch the same price as it does today. At that time bloodsnails were harvested in different places, including many of the islands of Valleria, and even as far west as the land of Longhorn. I heard that the Vallerian folk produced their dye by gathering the snails in large barrels and leaving them to rot in the sun. The stench filled the Vallerian archipelago for several weeks every summer. In the end the bloodsnails were wiped out completely. There were none left.

But our island still has a thriving colony. We have an alternative method of collecting the dye.

The snail harvest happens at the height of spring, after the awakening of the Spring Star. We perform rites of thanks in the Temple of the Rose in anticipation of the coming summer; we burn a huge bonfire of driftwood and branches blown down during the winter storms, and then we wait for a day of fine weather.

Bloodsnails are Sister Loeni's domain. She decides when to harvest, she organizes everything and oversees the dyeing process. She is also responsible for the trade, along with Sister Veerk. Her stern stare can force the price up sky-high. All that silver certainly does not just sit idly at the bottom of Mother's coffer. The novices who leave the Red Abbey and make their way back out into the world take silver with them so that they can do what they need to. Build infirmaries and found schools. Maybe improve lives in their homelands.

I thought about it sometimes. The silver I could take with me if I went back home to my mother and father. To my sister and brother. What I could do for them, and for my whole village. No more hunger winters. Shoes and thick furs for everybody. I thought about Anner; surely there are other children like her, ones who die from starvation.

But then I would have to leave the Abbey. Leave all my friends, leave the morning wash, Moon Dance, the lessons. Knowledge Garden, Sister Mareane's goat kids, the kittens.

Leave behind the security of never having to go hungry. Leave Sister O and the treasure chamber.

Sister Loeni thinks she is so superior because she is servant to the Blood. That gives her special responsibilities in the Temple of the Rose during the Blood rites, but that is no reason to be stuck-up. The servant to the Rose is the most important servant after Mother, but she is the most humble of all the sisters.

Toulan, Sister Loeni's novice, is a good friend of mine. I was very disappointed when she was called to become Blood novice last year. She and Sister Loeni are so different. Joem would have been much better suited! I thought Toulan would be terribly unhappy in her role. I certainly would be if I had to work with Sister Loeni every day. But when I showed sympathy for her fate, Toulan just smiled at me.

"Oh, I do not pay attention to all her lectures and chidings. When I finally stopped listening to them I heard everything that lies behind them. She has a lot of knowledge and she takes her role very seriously. She will not let the bloodsnails die out. And as servant to the Blood I get to explore some of the deepest mysteries of the First Mother."

Toulan has always been the most sensible of the novices. When the others would sneak away from praise to go swimming, or hide in the goat stalls to get out of some boring duty, Toulan would take no notice of them and get on with her duties patiently. She would never snitch, and it is not that she is boring, just serious. She saw her parents die of a terrible disease when she was little. Then she made a long and perilous journey to the Abbey all by herself. For a long time I thought she would become Sister Nar's novice. She is fascinated by herbs and healing. But she says she wants to delve deeper into the mysteries of the First Mother.

ᴡ

We were blessed with beautiful weather this spring. No sudden spring storm erupted, it was mild and pleasant, and when the Spring Star awoke White Lady was still wearing her crown of snow and her slopes were so covered with white fulcorn flowers that the whole mountain looked snow covered.

After we performed the rites of Revival and Mother made all the offerings, every morning dawned with perfect weather. But Sister Loeni still made a big deal of choosing the perfect day, with wind from the northeast, to ensure the harvest went as smoothly as possible.

Then, at last, one morning we were woken by the low clang of the Blood bell. I had warned Jai but she still bolted up in bed, terrified.

"It is the beginning of harvest week!" said Ennike. "No lessons!" She jumped out of bed and pulled Jai to her feet. "We get to be outside every day! No sun greeting, no washing, no boring duties!"

I smiled wryly at Ennike. No wonderful lessons, no meals at Hearth House, or evenings in the treasure chamber either. I was happy too, of course, but for different reasons. The snail harvest is the only work that all sisters and novices do communally and I love it when we all gather together. Even the sisters from the Solitary Temple accompany us. The only ones who stay in the Abbey are the oldest sisters, whose backs can no longer bend over snails and baskets.

We gathered in the courtyard in front of Hearth House. Sister Mareane and Dori had harnessed our two donkeys up to carts packed with neat coils of silk thread and woolen yarn. Toulan and Sister Loeni handed out baskets to everybody, even Mother, and then we left the Abbey via the goat door.

The island smelled of honey and dew as we walked up the path along the mountainside, and I remember thinking that I never could have dreamt of such a place when I lived in the village back home. A place with warmth and food and knowledge. Life in Rovas was like a cave where everybody is oblivious to the outside world, and the cold darkness of the cave is all anybody knows. Coming to the Abbey and learning to read was like opening up a big window and being flooded with light and warmth. I took a deep breath and felt grateful for the feeling of food in my belly, the sun on my face, and the fresh spring breeze around my legs. Happiness, I thought. This is happiness.

The sisters were walking in front of me in their worst, most worn-out and stained clothes, with trouser legs rolled up and ready. They were laughing and chatting and I could hear Sister O's deep voice stand out from the rest. Jai walked next to me with her fingers tightly clasping the handle of her basket, and Heo was jumping around behind me with her best friend Ismi, a little red-haired girl from Valleria, who has been with us since last summer. Behind them Ennike was singing a song with the junior novices.

> *The cat's asleep on the hot stone wall,*
> *Hop hop my little froggy!*
> *And the sun's ablaze like a golden ball,*
> *Hop hop my little froggy!*
> *The girl waits in her robe of red*
> *A crown of flowers round her head*
> *The wind horn blows its silver call,*
> *Hop hop my little froggy!*

I turned around to look at them. On every "hop hop" all the junior novices did a big frog leap along the path and exploded into giggles. The donkey carts were behind them and the older novices were right at the back with their headscarves flapping gently in the bright sunlight.

I turned to Jai.

"We will camp on the beach, at least for tonight. Maybe

longer if the weather stays this beautiful. Have you ever slept outside?"

"No. It was forbidden for girls to leave the house after sundown."

That was the first time she had mentioned her old life. I was so curious about what land she was from. At first I thought maybe Devenland, but Jai was too fair-haired to be from those parts. I did not dare ask.

"It can be a bit uncomfortable and I find it difficult to sleep the first night, even though I am tired from the day's work. But there are plenty of stars to stare at if you cannot sleep."

A low wall runs along the first stretch of the path. It protects walkers from falling down the steep slopes of the cliff where the Abbey is situated. Red-haired little Ismi came running past us and jumped up onto the wall. She stretched her hands out to the sides and walked along it fearlessly.

"Look at me! Now I am taller than all of you!" she said, laughing triumphantly. Before I had time to react Jai rushed over and lifted her down angrily.

"You could have fallen!" She leaned to look over the wall. Foaming white seawater crashed against the jagged boulders below.

Ismi just laughed and skipped out of our reach. Little girls tend to believe they are invincible, and Ismi is a particularly wild one.

Soon the steep path leveled out and we followed the south side of the mountain. We walked through the vineyards, where new leaves were just beginning to appear on the vines.

"This is where Sister Király and her novices grow grapes for raisins," I said, and pointed. "At some of the festivals we get raisins in our winter porridge. And our olive groves are down there in the valley, near the bay."

Jai shielded her eyes with her hand, dazzled by the sunlight on the water's surface.

"The sea is so big," she said, "and it is always changing color from one moment to the next. I could look at it forever and never get bored. And the horizon ... sometimes it is so sharp, like a knife edge, but at other times you can hardly see it through the haze of heat or rain."

"Was your home very far from the sea?"

She lowered her hand. "No. But I never got to see it. I never left my father's house and the rice fields in the valley. When I was very little I was allowed to go with them to Color Fest, but then my father decided that the girls had to stay at home."

So there must have been more children in Jai's family.

"I had never seen the sea either before I came to Muerio," I said. Jai looked at me questioningly. "That is the Vallerian seaport. The one that most of the girls who come here set sail from. I had seen quite big lakes on my journey south, but nothing could prepare me for the sea. It goes on forever. I was so scared when I boarded the boat!" I laughed at the memory, but Jai was serious.

"I was scared too. But not of the sea."

"Maresi!" Heo pulled me by the arm. "Maresi, tell us a story!"

I smiled at her earnest little face. "Heo, it is not polite to interrupt."

"Yes, but you just keep talking and talking. Ismi wants to hear a story too!"

"Shall I tell the one about White Lady and why she always wears a hat made of snow?"

"No, please Maresi, tell us the one about when the robbers attacked the Abbey!" Ismi grabbed me by my other arm. I glanced at Jai. That might not be such a good story for her to hear; it might frighten her. But it does have a happy ending.

"It was several years after the First Sisters landed on the island in the ship *Naondel*. They had already managed to build Knowledge House and Sister House, and were working on the Temple of the Rose. Sister House was much smaller then because there were only seven First Sisters. Do you remember their names, Heo?"

"Kabira, Clarás, Garai, Estegi, Orseola, Sulani and . . ." She bit her lip in concentration. "I never remember the last one."

"Her name was Daera and she was the first servant to the Rose." I moved my basket from one hand to the other and looked over at Jai. "Look, there is the path that goes north to the valley where we grow our crops between our Abbey and White Lady. From there the path leads to the Solitary

Temple, but we are following White Lady's southern slope down to the south coast of the island. It is flat there and good for harvesting snails."

"Carry on with the story!" whined Ismi.

"The Abbey did not have much silver in those days. The Sisters had not discovered the bloodsnail colony yet. They were too busy setting up the Abbey, building houses, and gathering more knowledge. I do not think there were any novices here then, but I am not sure. I do not think rumors about the Abbey had spread yet."

"But a ship came anyway!" said Heo. "A big one!"

"Yes, there came a big ship with a sharp bow and red and gray sails, a ship much like the *Naondel*. It does not say in any of the books I have read, but I think it might have come from the Eastern lands, like the First Sisters. There were bad men on the ship. They wanted to get at the First Sisters' knowledge. Maybe they wanted to get at the Sisters themselves."

Jai stumbled. I took her hand to help her up and kept hold awhile after she found her feet.

"That was before the outer wall was built, so the Abbey

was completely unprotected. The men sailed straight into the harbor one night while the Sisters were sleeping. But the island was not sleeping. When the men stepped on land all the birds on the island began to sing and woke the Sisters up. They ran to Knowledge House at once."

"Why did they go there, Maresi? Why didn't they go up in the mountains?"

"I don't know, Heo. Maybe they wanted to protect the knowledge from the men?"

"How can you protect knowledge?"

"If it is contained in books, for example. Now stop interrupting. The Sisters rushed into Knowledge House and the men surrounded the building. There were a lot of men and the Sisters were far outnumbered. The men had sharp swords, which gleamed in the moonlight. They tried to break into the house but they could not. When they tried to smash the windowpanes, it was as if the glass were made of stone. Then they tried to set fire to the house, and at first it seemed as if they had succeeded. The wood of the door and roof began to smolder and the men rejoiced. Soon the Sisters would burn inside, along with all their knowledge.

"But then a man who had stayed behind on the ship came to join them and when he saw the fire he became very angry. He yelled that their master wanted them to take the women's power and knowledge back to him. Their lives were of no consequence, but the knowledge could not go up in smoke. The men had to quench the fire at once."

"I have seen the marks," said Jai quietly, her eyes fixed on the path beneath her feet. "On the door to Knowledge House. The traces of the fire's flames will be there forever."

As she said this I realized that she was right. The bottom of the door is blackened with ancient soot.

"Then the men said that they would wait them out. The women would have to come out when they ran out of food and water. So the men sat down, crossed their legs and got ready to wait for as long as necessary."

"But then they saw them!" Heo could not hold it in any longer. "The Moon women!"

"That's right. While the men were sitting there with their swords in their laps, ready to slay the Sisters if they dared come out, they felt the earth suddenly begin to quake. On the mountain above the Abbey they saw seven giant women walking with great strides. The women were silver-white and looked as though they were made of moonlight, but the ground trembled and quaked under their steps. Their long, loose hair lashed against the mountainside, ripping up flowers and small trees. Then they began to shine all the stronger and, though the men turned their faces away in fear, the women's effulgence reflected in the shine of the men's swords and blinded them. When the men could no longer see, the seven giant women picked up huge boulders and hurled them down upon them. The rocks missed the Abbey buildings but hit the men and swept them down into the ocean."

We all went quiet for a while.

"They say that the ground where the men were standing ran red with blood." I glanced over at Jai. She was ghostly pale but calm. "The rocks that did not roll into the ocean became the foundation of the outer wall."

"Where did the giant women come from? The Sisters were in Knowledge House, weren't they?"

"I don't know, Heo. Maybe they were summoned by the

island itself. Maybe the First Sisters were capable of more than we know. It happened too long ago to know for sure."

Heo and Ismi scampered along the path, kicking at pebbles and shouting that they were giant women made of moonlight. Jai looked at me with a grave expression.

"Do you think the birds would still wake us? If somebody came?"

ꞗ

We reached the beach soon after midday. The sun was at her highest point in the sky, shining straight down on us. The south coast of the island is the only place without steep, plunging cliffs between mountain and sea, where White Lady's lowest slopes level off into rolling layers of rock that stretch down toward the water. The beach is shallow and perfect for snail harvesting. We sat down under a clump of harn trees to eat the bread and cheese Sister Ers and Joem shared out. Cissil, Sister Ers's other novice, went around with a stone jug of spring water that they had kept cool under the yarn skeins in the donkey carts. The soot marks on Cissil's cheeks were running with sweat from the long walk.

Then Sister Loeni called for our attention.

"Most of you know what to do. Jai and Ismi, watch the others. Fill your baskets with snails and then bring them up here to me and Toulan so we can show you how to do the dyeing. And be careful with the snails! They must not come to harm."

We all waded out into the cool ocean. The junior novices were jumping and laughing and the sisters were watchful and calm. Jai kept close to me and I showed her how to find where the bloodsnails live in small clusters stuck fast to the rocks, and how to carefully pry them loose and put them in the basket. The snails cling to the rocks with amazing strength, so it takes a long time to detach them without harming them.

"I thought they were red," said Jai, successfully lifting off her first snail. "They look as white as mother-of-pearl."

"The red is inside," I answered and laid the snail in my basket. "You will see."

When our baskets were full we carried them up to

the tree where Sister Loeni and Toulan had constructed a makeshift table of four long planks laid across the two donkey carts. The donkeys were grazing under the trees close by.

Toulan showed us where to put down the baskets, and then unrolled a spool of silk thread until the thread ran the length of the table three times. When the bloodsnails get scared they emit the precious red pigment that gives the snail its name. Sister Loeni handed Jai a snail and showed her how to frighten it by tapping on the shell with her nail and then wiping it along the threads immediately. As soon as the snail had emitted all of its color, we laid it in an empty basket and picked up the next one.

It is a slow way to dye thread. If we did it by the old Vallerian method, leaving the snails to die and rot in big barrels to extract the color, we could dye much more and earn much more silver. But then our bloodsnails would soon die out. Besides, the Abbey does not need so much silver.

When we had no snails left we carried the baskets and used snails a little farther up the beach. Then we tipped them carefully back into the sea. Our hands and arms were already tinged with red, and they were going to get redder still. After the dyeing a large part of the beach is always stained blood-red, and under the trees where Sister Loeni and Toulan hang up the threads and yarn to dry, the grass looks as if it is made of garnet.

ω

When evening came, Sister Ers and her novices served up food on the rocks: more bread and cheese and the delicious spiced meat pies filled with dried nirnberries that Sister Ers only ever bakes for the harvest. We ate with dark-red fingers, and the sisters lit two fires, one for them and one for the novices. We gathered around our fire and talked. The sun sank below the creamy layer of cloud resting over the western horizon and hung there like a golden ball. The ocean was a brilliant blue, dappled with darker streaks, and it whispered softly against the shore. The sky along the horizon was the color of ripe peaches, but above the thin layer of cloud it was bright blue, and the farther my gaze wandered upward, the darker it became. A single star was already out, directly above our heads. Some koan birds flew over the darkening sea with their distinct shrieking calls. Heo was sleeping with her head in my lap while the sun sank into the sea and the sky turned purple. The water shimmered lilac and turquoise like a wrinkled sheet of silk. Then, all the way down by the horizon, the Spring Star lit up, clear and cold.

My eyes felt heavy and my back ached from bending forward all day. The ocean's whispering song was like a sleepy lullaby. But I love to sit and watch the night sky come creeping across the sea, and I fought against sleep long after the other novices had wrapped themselves up in their blankets and settled down around the fire. Soon Jai was my only company. Her unwavering gaze was fixed on the deep-blue sky and her eyes shone black in the fire's fading glow.

"Is it not the most beautiful thing you have ever seen?" I asked her in wonder. "All this beauty makes me ache inside."

Jai nodded and swallowed, and then I saw that tears were spilling from her eyes. I carefully removed Heo's head from my knee and crawled over to Jai, though she did not seem as if she was going to have another screaming panic attack. She only sat facing the stars, crying and crying in stillness and silence. I took her hand and held it in mine. We sat like that for a long time while the night deepened around us. Eventually Jai spoke up to the stars.

"She will never get to see this. Unai, my sister. She will never get to see any of these beautiful and wonderful things I am experiencing here." She wiped her cheeks roughly with her free hand. "That is what I think about, Maresi. Everything she will never get to see or do."

"Is she dead?"

"She is dead. Dead and buried." Jai took her hand from mine and pressed it over her eyes. "Maresi, I saw them bury her. I saw my father and his brothers shovel earth over her bare face. I saw them stamp the earth down over the place where she lay. I saw them put down their spades and walk away to the village, to drink and celebrate. To celebrate that Unai was gone, celebrate that my good sister was not their problem anymore. They left us there next to her grave, my mother and me."

Many who come to this island have lost people they love.

I tried to take Jai's hand again, to show her that I understood and I shared her pain. But her fists were clenched and she was rigid and distant.

"Unai who had never done any harm to anyone! Unai who was the most obedient of daughters. She swore nothing had happened between her and the boy she had been seen talking to but Father did not believe her. She was on her way from the well and he'd asked her for a drink of water and she gave him some. She was always kind to everybody. She did not even know his name! But Father did not believe her, he called her a whore. The boy was of the Miho folk, not the Koho folk like us. That made it even worse. We are never allowed to mix with them. So Father said the family's honor was tainted. That she must die. I think about how it must have felt, Maresi." She sat up, turned toward me, and leaned her face close up to mine. Her large eyes were as black as coal in the darkness. "Every night when I go to bed I lie there feeling what she felt. My mouth full of earth. The weight of stone and soil on my lungs, my nostrils blocking up. Then soon I cannot breathe at all and I slowly suffocate to death while my family watches on, while my beloved sister watches on and does nothing to save me. Every night I am her, Maresi, every night I am Unai!"

I could not stop myself from recoiling in horror. "You mean," I said and heard myself splutter, "you mean that she—"

"She was alive when they buried her," whispered Jai. "And then they stamped on her grave."

ᛟ

The weather held out and we stayed at the beach all week. The harvest was good and Sister Loeni was pleased. Mother was with us most days, but she always went back to the Abbey at night to check on the oldest sisters who had not come with us. Sister Ers and her novices made the journey back and forth over the mountain several times with food for the snail-pickers, transported on the donkeys' backs.

Toward the end of the week the junior novices were losing patience. There were more and more occasions when I found myself running around looking for two or three of them who had gone off on their own down to the beach or into the woods. I would not force them to go back to work, but they had to stay in my sight while they played. The sea can be dangerous if you are not careful, and the woods are large and easy for little girls to get lost in.

One afternoon, as I was coming out of the woods leading Heo and Ismi by the hand, Mother came to meet us. I crouched down next to the girls.

"You must stay where I can see you. What if you got lost in the woods and missed supper? Think how hungry you would be. I know Cissil and Joem are bringing fresh cheese and jam buns today."

"You'd find us in time," said Heo with absolute certainty. "You always do."

She took Ismi by the hand and they ran giggling to play on the rocks. Mother shielded her eyes to watch them and I stood up. "I am sorry, Mother. I try to keep them in line but it is difficult when I am working at the same time."

I had been at the Abbey for many years but Mother had only spoken to me directly a handful of times. She has more important things to do than talk to novices.

"Has Sister Nummel entrusted the junior novices to you?" she asked, lowering her hand.

"No, Mother." I looked up. Mother turned her wrinkly face toward me. I had never noticed how long and thick her eyelashes were before.

"Yet you do it anyway. Why?"

I thought for a moment. "They like me. And they need me, I think." I smiled. "I need them. I do not miss my siblings as much when I can help others."

"You are thinking about your sister?"

Mother knew all about Anner. It was easy to forget sometimes, but she knew everything about the novices. I nodded. Maybe looking after the other little ones at the Abbey was my way of compensating for her death. I wanted to make sure nothing bad happened to them. I wanted to protect them like I could not protect Anner.

"You are helping Jai as well." It was a statement, not a question. I looked over at Jai to where she was bent double, walking along the edge of the sunlit sea.

"Ennike helped me when I first came. Now it is my turn."

"Has Jai told you what she has gone through?" Mother began walking along the edge of the woods, back to Sister

Loeni's dyeing table, and I followed behind. The mild sea breeze carried the sound of the junior novices' laughter. It smelt of seaweed and salt and trodden grass.

"Some. She will tell more when she is ready."

"You are important to her, Maresi. You must not abandon her."

I looked at Mother with surprise. Her tone had suddenly become very serious.

"Of course I will not, Mother."

"Good." She raised her hand in greeting to Sister Loeni and her voice sounded normal again. "Perhaps Sister Nummel will call you to be her novice. You are good with the children."

Sister Nummel? I had never considered it before. Maybe. I did get on well with her and we did often talk about the junior novices and their troubles. But it did not quite sit right in my gut. Of course I liked taking care of the little ones, but . . .

"You are already responsible for them, in any case." Mother turned to me, her voice low and intense again. Her eyes were the same bright blue as her headscarf. "If anything happens I want you to take care of the juniors, Maresi. I trust them in your safekeeping." She touched my forehead with one finger and I understood that her words carried great importance. I nodded solemnly. Mother regarded me awhile and then left without another word.

"What did Mother want?" asked Ennike curiously. She came walking up to me with an empty basket on her arm and Jai on her heels. I thought about how Mother had looked at me when she talked about Jai.

"I think Sister Nummel might call me to be her novice," I answered slowly.

"Would you like that?" asked Ennike. "You do enjoy being with the children."

"I think so." I looked at Heo and Ismi jumping along the water's edge, pretending they were riding invisible horses. Jai followed my gaze.

"I would like it too," she said, much to my surprise. "I like little children. I have three little brothers. I raised them at least as much as my mother did."

Ennike and I exchanged a glance. I had told her about Jai and Unai. I had not told anybody else, but seeing as Jai spent so much time with us, I thought it best that Ennike knew.

"You are welcome to help me with them," I said. "Let's go and see if we can get them to pick some snails before it is time to eat."

After harvest week Abbey life started up again as usual with lessons, rituals, and duties. We were looking forward to Moon Dance and the wonderful celebration feast afterward. At night I dreamed about pies and koan eggs.

Sister O's lessons focused on how the world works.

"There are many people throughout the known lands who worship false gods. They take heroes from legends and turn them into gods, or pray to giant sea monsters, or create gods in their own image and offer sacrifices to them." Sister O lectured us from the front of the classroom. Winds from the sea crept in through the open window, carrying the sounds of early summer: flies, seabirds screeching, the soft bleating of newborn kids up in the goat house.

"But it is the First Mother who gave life to the world and all power comes from her," continued Sister O. "Her energy flows through the earth like blood flows through our veins. There are certain people who leech off the lifeblood of the

First Mother, who take her power and use it for their own gain."

"But there are other ways to invoke the First Mother's power," said Ranna. She and her sister Ydda are both Sister Kotke's novices and their clothes are also always a little damp and wrinkled from the steam of Body's Spring. I like them. They are strong and not afraid of hard work, and though they mainly keep to themselves, they have always been friendly to me.

Ydda nodded to her sister. "In our homeland, Lavora, there is a legend about a girl who summoned the wind and tore up mountains with her singing. But she did not take anything from the First Mother. She worked with her."

"That legend is very old," said Sister O. "You are quite right. She learned to hear the First Mother's voice and sing in harmony with it. There are other stories, more recent ones, about women who have actually seen the First Mother. She has many different names and faces, but she exists everywhere, whatever she is called." Sister O pointed outside to the junior novices' classroom. "Little Heo is the descendant of an Akkade woman who helped the First

Mother take revenge on a man who had harmed her, and she saw one of her faces."

"How can someone use the First Mother's power?" asked Dori. Bird was pecking affectionately at her ear.

"All women have the First Mother in them," said Sister O. "There are many ways of invoking her power. Much of this knowledge is lost today. In the beginning we remembered more of our origin and perhaps had more of the First Mother in us." She raised an ominous finger. "But people have also exploited the First Mother's power, by tearing it out of the very ground we walk on."

"How can the First Mother let that happen?" Ennike sounded upset. "It is not right!"

"No it is not right, but the First Mother rarely gets involved in people's dealings with one another. We are responsible for ourselves and our own lives. That is the gift she has given us."

"How can the First Mother's power be torn out?" I asked. It did not sound possible.

"Nobody knows for sure. It is mentioned in the

First Sisters' scriptures, but those texts are difficult to understand. The First Mother's power had somehow been exploited and weakened in the Sisters' homeland. But, knowing that such knowledge is dangerous and nearly always used in the wrong way, the First Sisters wrote in riddles. People could take wealth and power for themselves and enslave others. They did not want just anyone to be able to read the scriptures and ascertain how to do this."

"Why can men not come to the island?"

It was the first time Jai had ever asked a question in class. All heads turned toward her, but Sister O did not seem to notice anything unusual.

"This is sacred ground. The First Sisters knew it as soon as they arrived. The First Mother's power is strong here. Her blood runs near the surface. In different parts of the world they worship different aspects of the First Mother. Some revere the Maiden, others the Mother, and a few people worship the Crone. Here we know the truth of the First Mother: she is all three. All of her sides are equally present here. The beginning, the continuation, and the end are all here. The First Sisters decided that men must not come here, perhaps to protect the Abbey, or perhaps for some other reason. It has been that way ever since. In the outside world there are rumors of a curse on any man who sets foot on Menos. We do nothing to dispel these rumors." Sister O gave a wry smile.

Jai leaned forward. "But what would happen if a man came here?"

"It has happened. When the thieves attacked the First Sisters," I answered quickly. "Remember the story I told?"

"It happened another time," said Sister O, to my surprise. "A lone man came here some generations ago. He sought protection and healing. The Abbey gave him refuge and cured his wounds."

Jai crossed her arms tightly. "Why? Why did the First Mother allow that? Why did the Abbey allow that?" Her voice was tense.

"Men are not our enemies, Jai. This man needed our help and we gave it of our own free will. We are the guardians of the First Mother's wisdom, but the wisdom is for the benefit of all."

ʊ

One day after lessons Sister O called me back just as I was about to leave the classroom. Jai stopped in the doorway and looked at us, but Sister O waved her away.

"You read every night in the library," she said. I nodded. Sister O looked out of the window at the sea. She always stands with bad posture and has to jut her chin out high in compensation so as not to look at the floor. Her neck makes the shape of an S. She looks like a skinny wading bird in a blue headscarf.

"Can you read all the books?"

"No. Not the oldest ones that the First Sisters wrote in their own language and brought with them from the Eastern lands."

"Would you like to learn to read them?" Sister O turned to me.

I would often look at the ancient books and scrolls and wonder what they contained. I hate not being able to read everything I see. It is like some wonderful secret right in front of my face, or a bit of delicious spiced meat pie that is pulled away every time I reach out my hand. I nodded eagerly.

"Oh yes! I have always wondered what kind of knowledge the First Sisters brought with them."

"Much of it has been written about in other books since."

"But you always say that an interpretation is never the same as learning something for yourself!"

Sister O smiled drily at my eagerness.

"If you are seriously interested I can teach you the basics of the language. That means that you would have one or two lessons with me, in my chamber I think, after the normal lessons of the day. Could you manage that?"

"Can we start straight away?" I went up to Sister O and would have taken her hand and dragged her to her chamber right then if I had dared. "Please?"

"Hm. I have to ask Mother first. But if she gives her blessing we can start tomorrow."

ω

Mother had no objections to the proposal, so the next day I started my lessons in the Eastern tongue with Sister O. Jai did not want to be alone and she refused to go anywhere while I was with Sister O. Instead she sat outside in the

Temple Yard and waited until I was finished. Often Heo or one of the cats would keep her company.

When I first came to the Abbey I learned the coast language because I had to. It was scary not being able to understand what people were saying around me. I did not have any language lessons but had to absorb everything I heard as quickly as possible. This time, however, I was learning out of curiosity, not necessity. I was very disappointed to discover that it was a much harder and slower process this time, without hearing the language all around me. Sister O did not know how the words were pronounced; it was a written language we had to contend with. I felt as if it was taking forever to understand the texts, but Sister O scoffed at my complaints and muttered that she did not understand how it was possible that I could learn so fast.

I spent every evening in the treasure chamber trying to decipher the most ancient books. At first I could only recognize a few words here and there, but as the moon shifted phase I understood more and more. When I came to a word I did not understand I would run across the

Temple Yard to Sister House and ask Sister O. She always complained about the intrusion but she would answer my questions. She is good like that, Sister O. Sister Loeni often dismissed questions with a frown and a "Not now, Maresi" or "You ask too many questions, Maresi." Sister O might grumble and tell me to stop disturbing her, but she always gave me an answer.

There were so many exciting books to delve into. Sister O was right when she said that a lot of it was written about in newer books I had read. But it all sounds so different expressed in the ancient and poetic Eastern language. There are more details. Besides, it is wonderful simply being able to read words written by the First Sisters themselves. I had been hearing about the First Sisters ever since I came here, the entire history of the Abbey was suffused with them. Now they were coming to life.

There is a short text just about blood, written by Garai, the one who planted Knowledge Garden. It contains a section describing which plants fortify the blood, which staunch blood flow, and which can delay a woman's moon blood. One chapter talks about the First Mother's blood, how it courses through the world, techniques to tap into it and the risks involved. It also says the First Mother's blood can be made through mixing the blood of the three aspects of the Triple Goddess. That chapter is difficult and I did not understand much. Another chapter is about women's wisdom blood and its possible uses. It explains which rituals should only be carried out by women who retain their wisdom blood. When I asked Sister O what wisdom blood was, she replied drily that the First Sisters believed moon blood had magical powers.

One particularly ancient-looking scroll tells the story of the First Sisters' escape from their homeland, Karenokoi, the many hardships of their journey and their eventual arrival at Menos, when their ship was hurled onto the island by a huge storm. I had heard the story many times, but this version revealed something new.

"Here follows a written account of the events that followed the landing of the *Naondel* on the island of Menos with the seven sisters from Karenokoi on board. Our names are Kabira, Clarás, Garai, Estegi, Orseola, Sulani and Daera, and Iona who has been lost but who will forever be a part of us and of our strength." I never knew there was an eighth. Iona.

Another book was entirely about hair, which I found strange. There was a whole section on combs—which must be made of copper when they are used to invoke the wrath of the First Mother. There are lots of books about healing, some about the building work at the Abbey, and many others that were not written by the Sisters themselves. There is one about how to manipulate the world, but it is much too difficult for me to understand. There is a whole stack of books about the history of the Eastern lands. I pored through them hungrily, trying to imagine what these far-off lands and folk might look like.

One evening, on my way to the treasure chamber, I passed by the door to the crypt in Knowledge House and realized I could read what was written on it. The writing is in the Eastern tongue and, though I had always known what it meant, it was the first time I could read it for myself: *Here lie seven sisters, united in work and in love*, it says. Simple but beautiful words. Then all seven names are inscribed: Kabira, Clarás, Garai, Estegi, Orseola, Sulani and Daera.

At the bottom is something I had always thought was only a decorative symbol, but now I could see it was actually an embellished *I*. *I* for Iona.

The crypt door does not look like a door. The corridor running through Knowledge House is decorated with half-columns that curve out of the walls, and the text is embossed in the space between two columns. There is no visible hinge or handle, and if you do not know what the text says, it would just look like a decoration. But it is a door and it leads down to the most sacred place on the island, where the Crone reigns. I would always hurry past the door as quickly as I could. The Crone presides over wisdom and death, and so naturally her sacred place would be the burial chamber beneath Knowledge House. Wisdom is very important to me, of course, but I have had more than enough dealings with death.

During the hunger winter a silver door appeared in our house and stayed there day and night. No one else in my family could see it and I never told them about it. At the time I did not know what was on the other side, waiting for me with insatiable hunger, a hunger even greater than the one ravaging my body. The Crone. The door handle was shaped like a snake with eyes of black onyx, and that snake slithered and hissed through my starving delirium. The door only disappeared once the Crone had gotten what she wanted.

She wanted a life. She wanted Anner.

I can still feel Anner's frail little body in my arms. How little she weighed at the end. I can hear Mother's quiet sobs and see Father hunched over the casket he had crafted out in the shed.

I had feared the Crone ever since and the crypt was the only place on the whole island that filled me with dread.

ʊ

Jai accompanied me every evening while I read from the ancient scrolls. Sometimes I read aloud to her and she listened with interest and asked questions.

Jai had relaxed somewhat after that night on the beach when she had told me about her sister. She was confident enough to speak without being spoken to, at least with people she felt comfortable with like me, Ennike and Heo.

We learned a few crumbs of information about her early life. Her three younger brothers were called Sorjan, Doran, and Vekret. Her mother had had several miscarriages after having Jai and gave up hope of ever giving her husband sons. After Vekret was born her father was finally satisfied and left his wife's bed for good. The night when he moved out Jai and Unai heard their mother crying. When they asked her the next morning if she missed her husband terribly, she smiled through the tears. "No. I am happier than I have ever been."

We found out that Jai hated it in autumn when they had to make the preserves: the air in the kitchen was sharp with vinegar vapor and she had to dice the vegetables ever so thinly. But she did enjoy crushing her mother's various spice blends in a mortar.

She had never seen snow, so when Heo and I tried to explain what it was she burst out laughing for the first time since we had known her. She has a surprisingly light laugh considering how deep her voice is. "Something cold and white that falls from the sky! You do say the funniest things, Heo."

"Have you not seen the white snow cap on White Lady?" I asked with an exasperated smile. Jai shook her head and I understood that, as far as she was concerned, the mountain peak could just as well be covered in white flowers or stones.

My least favorite time in spring is when we come down to Body's Spring one morning and see Sister Kotke waiting there with a big grin. "Time for spring cleaning," she says, clearly taking pleasure in our groans.

Straight after breakfast all the novices gather with perpetually damp Sister Kotke in the central courtyard. Sister Kotke, Ydda, and Ranna have everything prepared: the big washing tubs, a fire in the stone pit near the well, a big iron pot of water hung above the fire.

"You know what to do," says Sister Kotke, and we hurry away to Novice House and Sister House to get all the bed linen we can lay our hands on, ripping off the sheets and emptying the cupboards. Then we stumble back to the central courtyard with our arms full and spread everything out on the clean-swept stone paving. Next Sister Kotke, Ydda, and Ranna go through all the sheets and cloths to decide which are acceptable, which need to be patched and repaired, and which are only good for rags. They sort it all into big piles while we deal with the water pot. As soon as the water bubbles Ennike and I carry the pot to one of the washing tubs and empty it very carefully so we do not scald ourselves with the boiling-hot water. Sister Kotke places the laundry into the tub in batches with her water-wrinkled hands before cutting in a piece of soap. Some novices stir it around with long washing paddles, which are whitened and smooth from years of use, while other novices haul more water up from the well to refill the pot.

I think laundry is the dullest task imaginable. Usually Sister Kotke and her novices do it all themselves, but not the spring wash. When at last everything has been boiled we load it onto a wagon and pull it down to the sea. There everything is scrubbed on beach stones and, finally, rinsed in the sea. After that the laundry is hung up to dry in the sun and the sea breeze, and we can eat and rest for a bit while it dries. Once it is dry, we sit there with needle and thread to patch and mend anything that is worn and tattered. I think that might be even more boring than the washing.

Jai and I were sitting side by side on a bench in the shade of Body's Spring, patching tears in the freshly washed linen sheets. I thought it might do her good to talk about her sister, so I plucked up my courage.

"Tell me about Unai," I said, biting off a thread. "What was your sister like?"

Jai's hand froze for a moment, but then she continued to sew. I let out a breath I had not realized I had been holding in. I was still worried I might frighten her away; incite the fear and horror that seized her when Heo asked about Unai before.

"Unai was two years older than me. Like all men my father had wanted a son as his firstborn. We were a disappointment to him." Jai turned the sheet around on her knee to continue sewing. "Unai was always a good daughter. She tried to be exactly the kind of Koho girl my father wanted: good, obedient, out of sight. She wanted to please him. And I wanted to be just like her." She put down her sewing and looked out over the courtyard with a vacant stare. "The best part of the day was just before the men came home from the rice field. If we'd already finished our daily chores, Unai and I would sit up on the roof. Sometimes Mother joined us if she had time. Our soma was so cold that our drinking bowls sweated in the warm evening air. Soma is a very refreshing drink made of mint, sugar, and a small, sour fruit called cerre that grows wild up in the mountains. We would sit there as the sun set behind the mountains and talk and laugh while we still could. Father did not like the sound of women laughing." She smiled faintly.

"No, the best time was probably at night when Unai and I would crawl into the bed we shared. First we helped each other take down our hair." She gave the back of her head a self-conscious little stroke. "Koho women wear their hair up. We could never be seen with our hair hanging loose like we do here. The higher the hair, the better. It takes a long time to take it all down at night. It is easier if you have someone to help. Then when we got into bed Unai would tell me what I had done well that day and what I could do better. At the same time she would massage my scalp, which ached from having my hair pulled so tight all day. Unai truly wanted me to be a good woman. One who followed all the traditions and was obedient and submissive so that Father could be pleased with us both. I so wanted him to be pleased with me, but only for her sake. I would do anything Unai asked me. But I could not be as submissive as she was. It seemed natural for her to bow her head and not make eye contact with Father, or any other men, and to answer, 'Yes, Father,' no matter what insults he threw at her. When he hit her she said it was her own fault. She was not quick enough or she had not been careful enough. I never felt that way." Jai looked at me. "It was difficult for me to be obedient. Everything inside me was fighting against it. But I did my best for Unai's sake. If Father was not satisfied with me, sometimes he took his anger out on her instead of me. But I could never believe it was my own fault that he resorted to the cane." She turned to me. "Did your father hit you if you did not bring his soma quickly enough? If the food was not to his liking, or if you accidentally spilled something when you were waiting on him and your brother?"

I shook my head. "My father would never have hit me or any of my siblings. And I have never waited on anybody."

Jai's eyes grew wide. "I always thought that was how it was for everyone. Unai was convinced that our lives would be easier if we could learn to live up to Father's expectations."

She closed her eyes, bowed her head, and swallowed hard. "She was a good daughter her whole life. It was of no use to her, in the end." Her voice became so little that I could barely hear her. "She did not even try to get out when he laid her in the pit. She could have gotten out, could have fought back. He threw earth on her body first. Saved the head until last, so that she would meet her death with open eyes. She still did not move until the weight of earth on her chest became too much. When she could not breathe panic set in and then she tried to struggle. But it was already too late."

I dropped the white sheet and threw my arms tightly around Jai. I could not even begin to understand such evil, that there were places in the world where people could do such things to one another.

"Holy Goddess," I whispered into Jai's hair, which smelled like soap and sun-bleached linen. "Maiden, Mother, Crone, I pray to all your aspects. Relieve this girl's burden."

Jai straightened up, shook my arms away, and looked at me. Her brown eyes glared beneath her sharp eyebrows. "I do not need relief, Maresi. But do pray for me. Pray that I will get my revenge."

She was frightening me. Her pain and anger were beyond anything I could understand. I grieve for Anner too, but I have never had a desire for revenge. I looked away and bent down to pick up my sewing from the ground.

"How did you get here?" I asked.

"Mother." Jai looked at the sheet on her lap, confused, as if she did not know how it had gotten there. "When she lost Unai she decided to stand up to Father for the first time in her life. She came into my room the night after they buried Unai. I was awake but I did not understand at first. She had packed up all her jewelry, and Unai's and mine, in a bundle. She dressed me and hid the jewels under my clothes and did my hair up without saying a word. Then she led me outside to where a man was waiting with a donkey cart. I do not know how she had gotten hold of such a thing. I did not ask. 'You are going to the Abbey,' she said. 'You will be safe there. I will lose another daughter, but you will be saved.'

"We had heard about the Red Abbey in stories and songs that Mother and our aunts sang to us sometimes when the men were not around. I always thought it was a myth. It sounded so unbelievable. A place filled only with women where men were not allowed. I could not imagine how they would get by. How they would survive. I was taught that a woman is nothing without a man.

"I do not know if Mother even believed the Abbey was anything more than a myth. But she knew that without Unai I could never live up to Father's expectations. And someone who has killed once does not hesitate to do it again." Jai closed her eyes. "She said nothing else. Only kissed me on the forehead and pushed me away. She did not stay to watch the cart drive away."

Jai opened her eyes. She looked up at the blue morning sky and straight into the sun as if to burn something clean from her eyes. "We were on the road all night and only let the donkeys rest briefly the following afternoon. The driver seemed very nervous. I think Mother paid him to drive me all the way to the sea, but he left me in the first town we came to. I do not even know what it was called. The driver was probably scared that my father might take revenge, because when we were on a little side street, all of a sudden he shooed me off the wagon and drove away without looking back. I stood on the street surrounded by strangers with no idea where I was or where to go. I was so scared, Maresi. I had never spoken to any men other than my male relatives before. I was so alone. I had always had Unai by my side." She lowered her face to her sewing and began to stick the needle in the cloth as if at random. "It was a woman who saved me. Of the Joi folk, no less. But when she saw me standing there she told me that a woman of my class shouldn't be seen in town alone without a male chaperone, and I started to cry. She took me into her house, which was small and modest but not dirty and unholy, as I'd been told Joi houses were. It was clean and respectable. I told her everything, because what else could I do? Even she knew about the Abbey. I'd always thought Joi folk were ignorant and did not know about anything except menial labor. She gave me some of her own clothes and dressed me like a Joi woman. When she let my hair down it was the first time anyone other than my mother or Unai had seen me with my hair undone. She told me to sew my jewelry into the hem of the chemise and I hid one ring on my body. She gave me food and board, but when I offered to pay she was offended. The next day her brother came and took me out of the town and nobody stopped me or talked to me, because what was there to see or say about a lowly Joi woman?

"Then I started walking. Sometimes I got a ride on some farmer's cart or a trading caravan for a little bit. I'd never walked so much in my life and my feet started bleeding, but then the skin hardened and I could walk some more. In the next town I stopped in a boarding house for Joi farmers where I rested a few days and ate my fill. But then one night I was robbed. May whoever did it die unmourned and forgotten and buried in an unmarked grave! After that the ring I'd hidden was the only thing I had. I had to walk the final stretch to the harbor city where I eventually found a sea captain willing to take me here in exchange for the ring. I am sure the sailors would have abandoned and robbed me also, if they had not known the Abbey might pay even more when they got me here. And Mother did pay generously."

"Were you not hungry? Afraid?"

Jai's hand trembled but carried on sticking the needle in the cloth. "The whole time."

A deep-red dot seeped through the linen sheet under Jai's hands. I gasped when I saw that it was not the cloth that she had put the needle in. She was stabbing at her left hand over and over again with the sharp point of the needle. When I held her hands back she hissed at me like a wounded animal.

"You realize she is gone now, right? Maresi, she is dead. My mother is dead! Father would never have let her live."

At the second full moon after the awakening of the Spring Star, moon and star come into alignment and it is time for Moon Dance. It is the most important of all the rites of the Abbey. It is when we visit the First Mother in her own realm and she meets us with all three aspects: Maiden, Mother, and Crone. Moon Dance honors the First Mother and we dance for the fertility of the world and the inseparable union of life and death. Mother always explains this to us the day before the dance.

ᚹ

We undressed on the beach. The night was cloudless and the moon was high in the sky, gazing down on us from amongst her starry entourage. The moon who rules the movements of water and women's blood, the moon who gives energy to all that lives and grows, the moon who measures time and reigns over death. The moon in whose image woman was created, the Moon, the Goddess, who hears our sorrows and shares our joy.

We stood in a line, alternating sisters and novices, and Mother took her position at the front and began to sing. It was a wordless, wailing song that carried over the bay and encircled us as we walked along the beach, toward the cape that encloses the bay to the south. Mother led us around the cape to Maidendance, a labyrinth of smooth, round stones of the same sort found along the beaches. It is there all year, eternal and strong, but we only go there once a year at Moon Dance.

Burning torches were stuck into the earth encircling the labyrinth. They made the surrounding darkness deeper still. When I looked up the Moon appeared larger than before, as if Mother's song had brought her closer. It was a brisk night and the stones were chilly beneath my feet, but I did not feel the cold. Mother's song kept me warm.

Mother was the first to dance into the labyrinth and out again. Maidendance is not a labyrinth to get lost in. It is a labyrinth to lead us into the other realm. Where life and death are one, and the Goddess herself resides. Mother lifted her feet up high, took big steps and carefully avoided touching the stones that formed the labyrinth. Touching them brings very bad luck. Mother has danced the Moon Dance for many years and never touched a stone. She came to a stop when she reached the middle and started spinning around slowly while her song turned into words. Words about the Goddess, words of the Goddess. Words that lauded and praised, cowered and trembled, saw and foresaw. They were hard to catch and fully understand. I could hear her singing about danger, singing about blood, about lifeblood and spilled blood, and shadows coming ever closer.

One by one sisters and novices weaved their voices into the song and danced through the labyrinth. Everybody danced in their own way and everybody added something new to the song. Voice after voice joined in with the song of worship, making it swell and grow like the ocean tide. But only Mother sang with the voice of the Goddess herself.

When Jai's turn came and the labyrinth pulled her in she raised her hands in terror at first, but then the Moon called to her and opened her mouth, and she joined her song in with the others'. Her fair hair reflected the moonlight and torchlight, shining gold and silver at the same time. Her body looked very thin and her scars glowed red against her white skin. As soon as she took the first step her hands flew out to the sides and she began to spin. Slowly at first, a little way into the labyrinth, but then with more and more force. The swing of the song went on. How could she not touch a stone if she kept spinning like that? I was the only one left who had not sung yet and I wanted to rush in and stop Jai. But Mother carried on singing loudly and steadily while the women and the girls lowered their voices and sang Jai through the labyrinth. She was spinning so quickly her hair whipped her in the face, and her movements became a blur. When she reached the middle she sped up even more, which I would not have thought possible. She spun until the sand whirled around her feet, until the torch flames flailed, until the Moon came down and kissed her flying hair. Sisters and novices sang and sang and Jai sang too, and together they all sang her out of the labyrinth again.

She had not touched a single stone.

My turn came last. When I took the first step of the dance my voice burst into song involuntarily. I heard it ringing in my ears but I was not aware of my mouth forming sounds. I felt the warmth of the torch flames on my skin, but I could not see them. All I saw was the Moon.

She was enormous now. So close that if I stretched out my hand I could touch her cool cheek. She filled my whole vision, filled me with her music. Now I understood: it was about life and death. I gave up my body to the song and let it dance me into the labyrinth.

I had danced this dance before and always felt the Moon's energy flood over me and leave me feeling wild, empowered, and free. But this time it was different. The Moon was bigger than ever before. Her energy was making the air vibrate. The moonlight pulsed so that everything around me seemed to flicker. The women outside the labyrinth, the rocks around us, the dark sea—everything was blurred and warped, like looking through the bottom of a bottle of Vallerian wine. The song continued to steer my steps and each one was solid and precise; I did not touch a stone.

Something loomed large in the center of the labyrinth. In the vibrating, trembling night it was the only thing whose form was fixed and clear.

It was a door, tall and narrow and silver in the bright moonlight. It was closed, but I could sense the darkness that waited on the other side. Darkness so deep not even the light of the Moon could penetrate it. It was the door from the hunger winter, and behind it the Crone was waiting.

I was gripped by a fear that cut through the trance and the song, and I tried in vain to stop my steps. The dance was taking me closer and closer to the door. I could not tear my eyes away from it. I had never seen it so clearly before. I could see that the frame was blackened with age, but the surface of the door was shimmering. I could see the handle, shaped like a snake with onyx eyes. The door was all too familiar. I did not want to see it, I did not want to acknowledge it existed, but my eyes refused to look away and my legs refused to obey me. A stream of air flowed out through the crack underneath the door and coiled around my calves. The rancid breath of the Crone. It mixed with the metallic smell of blood from my own skin. The smell of death that has clung to me for years, ever since the hunger winter. Since the Crone took Anner.

My jaws ached from trying to hold back the song and my body jerked from the strain of trying to stave off the dance. I was getting closer, so close that the tentacles of darkness were licking at my body. They were creeping out through the cracks around the door, luring and drawing me in. I could not resist. Nobody can resist death.

Then I heard the voice. It came floating through the darkness; it was made of darkness. Fragmented words stretching out to me.

Maresi. My daughter. Here, see my gateway. My mouth.

I danced on the threshold as the voice of the Crone scratched at my bones.

This is your House, said the Crone, and the terror became so great that I finally found my voice.

"I do not want to!" I screamed.

As soon as I broke the song the music cut out, the moonlight paled and the door disappeared. Clarity returned to the world.

"I do not want to!" I screamed over and over again until Mother appeared in front of me in the labyrinth and laid her hands on my body.

After that I remember no more. When I awoke I saw that Mother had carried me out of the labyrinth. The torchlight flickered around us and the moon was back to being a little lamp up in the heavens. Mother's concerned face was hovering above mine.

In the corner of my eyes I could see slicks of darkness sliding around, and on them rode the voice of the Crone, wordlessly whispering.

I did not join in with the celebration feast in the Moon Yard. I lay in bed in the dormitory trying to forget what I had seen and heard. I tried to sleep. I must have drifted off around dawn because I was woken up at midday by Sister O.

"Mother wants to talk to you. Do you feel strong enough yet?"

She gave me a piece of bread to eat and watched while I got dressed. My movements were slow. I did not want to talk to Mother. I did not want to answer any questions. I did not want to think about what had happened. But I could not say no to a direct summons from Mother herself. So I followed Sister O across the central courtyard and up Moon Steps. It had never felt as long a way as it did that day. The sun was shining in the bright-blue spring sky, the sound of junior novices playing came from the Knowledge Yard and I could see the goat kids frolicking gleefully up on the mountainside. The smell of the Crone's breath still lingered in my nostrils. Her voice mumbled in every sharp-edged shadow. I walked as closely behind Sister O as possible. The Crone could not take me if I was not alone.

Though I knew that if she wanted something, she would get it in the end.

Moon House is a low gray building with the Moon Yard beside it. The house is built of stone, like all houses on the island, and its back wall is formed by the mountain itself. The door is made entirely of metal. The surface might have been clean once, but it has accumulated dents and scratches since, which look like the result of many blows. It smells rancid. I had only ever been through it once before, when I arrived and was brought to Mother for the first time.

Mother was sitting behind her large desk, waiting for me. The sharp wind up on the mountainside made her chamber very cool. There were two doors in the room: one into the cell where Mother slept and another simple wooden door with iron fittings and a hefty knob. The first was ajar and I could see that it led into a naked little cell. There was a narrow, comfortable-looking bed, a desk with a lamp and a little window.

Mother's face was calm and expressionless, but I thought I could see a glimmer of worry in her bright eyes. I tried not to meet her gaze. I did not want her to guess the truth from my eyes. Sister O stood next to me, her back straight and her lips pressed tightly together. I had never seen her back straight before.

"Maresi, what happened last night?" Mother's voice was authoritative. She was expecting an answer.

I looked down at the ground. I could not lie to Mother. I could only stay silent.

"It was the Moon, was it not?" Mother's voice softened. "She can be frightening. I understand that. The first time she spoke to me I was also afraid. Afraid of the responsibility. I understood that she had chosen me as her servant. As Mother of the Abbey I stand closest to Havva. But before I was chosen as Abbey Mother I was called by the Moon. Maybe you were thinking about a different path, Maresi, but if you have been chosen by the Moon you cannot refuse. You must become my novice."

I looked up. Mother had not seen the door, had not heard the Crone. I did not know what to say. It was a great

116

honor to be invited to Moon House, but it was not right. Yes, the Moon had looked at me, but it was the Crone who spoke to me. Or were they one and the same? I glanced over at Sister O but I did not dare answer.

Mother's eyes impelled me to speak.

"The Goddess . . . she has three aspects, has she not? The Maiden, the Mother, and the Crone." Mother nodded encouragingly, so I dared to ask my question. "What about the Moon, is she one of them?"

Sister O sighed. "Now, Maresi. I have explained this before . . ." Mother raised a hand and cut her off.

"No, Maresi. The Moon is all three. The Moon is the face of the Goddess's unity."

"Then I was not called by the Moon," I said firmly. "That much I know."

I could not read Mother's expression. Was it disappointment I saw in her eyes?

"Are you absolutely sure?"

I nodded.

"Do you want to tell me what happened during the dance?"

I shook my head. I did not want to talk about it ever. I did not want even to think about it.

Mother gestured to dismiss us. Sister O followed close on my heels and I could feel her sharp gaze on my back. Mother had accepted my answer, but I knew it would not placate Sister O.

When we came down to the central courtyard I turned my face toward the sun. Sun, giver of life. I wanted her light and warmth to chase away the remainders of darkness inside me, but I also did not want to look Sister O in the eye. She stood next to me with her arms crossed and eventually I had no choice but to look at her.

"Maresi. If you tell me what happened maybe I can help you." She stretched out a hand and gave my headscarf an awkward little stroke. "You have always been able to come to me with your questions. If there is something you are wondering about or want to know . . ."

I shook my head again and sealed my lips tightly. She looked at me for a long time and sighed.

"Very well. But I am here if there is ever anything you want to talk about."

I watched her as she walked up the steps to the Temple Yard. Sister O had never asked me for more questions before.

ʊ

The next few days were difficult. I withdrew from the other girls because I was not willing or able to answer their questions. I stayed out in the sun as much as possible. All darkness scared me. Wherever shadows gathered I thought I could sense the door to the other realm. The realm of the Crone. Shadows seemed to be everywhere. The sun did not feel as bright as before. Everything was darker. In every gust of wind and every ocean whisper, I expected to hear the voice of the Crone.

It seemed that my uncertainty and weakness made Jai stronger. She became assertive and started speaking to the other novices, not only me and Ennike. Maybe she had to become strong because I was weak; to have the strength to support me for a while. She never asked me any questions but she was there for me whenever the darkness closed in. Often it happened in the mornings, when the sun was low and the shadows between the houses were deep and sharp as a knife's edge. When I least expected it the Crone's voice would drift toward me, whispering and hissing until I quaked with fear. Jai was always by my side, and she would take me back out into the sunshine and talk to me softly and sweetly, like I did for her when she first came to us. Her voice drove the Crone's voice away. For a while.

I never felt safe from the Crone's beckoning, but nights were the worst. It was then that the darkness pressed against my chest and eyes and I heard Anner's final rasping breath over and over again. Death's realm felt so near and my own heartbeat felt so unsteady and weak. How could I resist the will of the Crone? How could I keep myself away from her door?

Whenever the anxiety became too much, without a word or even a sound a hand came through the darkness and touched mine. Jai. She did not take hold of my hand but let me grip hers, if I wanted. I clutched her hand hard with my thumb on her wrist and her steady pulse mixed with mine to anchor me in this world.

With Jai's hand in mine I could sleep at last.

After a few days of bright sun my memories of darkness started to fade away and I could breathe again. I ceased to hear the Crone everywhere. I played and laughed as usual, took part in lessons and duties and went to the treasure chamber in the evenings to read. The only place where I felt uneasy was at the door to the crypt. I could feel the Crone's power emanate from it and always ran past as fast as I could. Now I was more than happy to have Jai's company. I was afraid of wandering around Knowledge House alone.

One morning after lessons Ennike, Jai, and I were sitting by the well in the central courtyard as the servant to the Rose came walking past. She stopped and smiled at us. I always feel shy around her. The servant to the Rose is the only sister who does not wear a headscarf, and her long copper-brown hair tumbles down her back in thick, gleaming locks. Her large eyes are dark and full of warmth and her fair skin was already covered in freckles from the strong spring sun. She is the most beautiful woman I have ever seen.

Whoever acts as servant to the Rose gives up her own name, so I do not know what she was called before she became the Rose. It is another name for the Maiden, the part of the First Mother whose wisdom is to do with the beginning of life and the sacred powers of the female body. In many communities the Maiden is merely a representation of innocence, but at the Abbey we know better. All the deepest mysteries of femininity belong to the Maiden. She is the seed and the sprout. The Mother, Havva, is life and fruitfulness, and the Crone is death and destruction. The Rose walked over to us.

"I have no novice, as you know. Could you three help me with something? I need to polish the Temple's sacred items before the summer rites, and some helping hands would be very welcome."

"Naturally." Ennike was on her feet at once. She did not seem to be as shy around the Rose as I was. Jai and I followed Ennike and the Rose up Eve Steps to the Temple of the Rose.

The door to the Temple of the Rose is the most beautiful one on the whole island. It is a double door, as tall as three women, and made of snow-white marble, with a rose pattern inlaid in red marble. We stopped in front of the door and I ran my fingers along its smooth surface. There was not a single join to be felt.

"Nobody does handicraft like this anymore," said the Rose.

"I wish there were a sister who knew this art, and that she could pass her knowledge on to me and me alone," I said, stroking the glossy surface again. The Rose smiled.

"Sister O has told me about you, Maresi. She was certainly right."

I felt myself turn bright red and quickly pulled my hand away. I was not entirely sure what she meant by that, but it was not unkind.

The Rose unlocked the doors and we stepped into the cool shade of the Temple.

As far as I can recall I had only been in there for thanks and praise. Now the Temple was empty and quiet. The two large rose-colored windows on the long east and west walls cast their rose-red light in beautiful patterns on the floor.

In the middle of the hall is a double row of slender columns stretching up into the ceiling shadows. The Temple is completely bare; there are no benches or chairs, no tables or ornaments. The only decoration apart from the rose windows is the marble floor, which is like a red and white woven carpet full of hidden vines, flowers, leaves, and swirls. The pattern they form almost looks like written words, and when I stare at it for long enough I feel as if at any moment I might crack the code and understand what it means. But I have not deciphered it yet.

At the far end of the hall, on the left-hand side, is the platform where the Rose stands to lead ceremonies. The Rose walked over to it, went up the wide marble steps, and waved for us to follow. Our steps echoed in the empty hall and it almost felt as if we were intruding somewhere we had no right to be. When I took the first step up the stairs I felt an unseen hand hold me back. I stopped and next to me Jai did the same. Ennike was oblivious and carried on up the steps. The Rose turned and looked at us. Her eyes lingered on Ennike. Then she raised her hand.

"I invite these daughters of the First Mother to tread

on the sacred ground of the Rose," she said, with the same formal voice she used in the big ceremonies, like the Blood rites and the unfurling of the Rose. The invisible hand let go and Jai and I were able to continue up the stairs.

The Rose opened the carved rosewood double doors at the back of the platform. We followed her into a room overflowing with objects.

The only light came from a single, narrow, north-facing window, but the light was reflected by hundreds of shining trinkets and nearly dazzled me. There were brass and silver candlesticks as tall as me. There were tables piled with dishes, bowls and boxes of every imaginable shape and size, all made of silver and gold. Nearly everything bore the emblem of a five-petaled rose. There were large old chests made of darkened wood, with tarnished fittings and locks, that looked as if they had not been moved for many decades. Cupboards lined the walls, some simple and others richly decorated with embossing and inlays. Some cupboard doors were ajar, revealing shelves stacked with yet more things: jewelry, boxes, cups, bowls, and heaps of objects I could not distinguish.

The Rose moved effortlessly amongst all the furniture and objects without touching or bumping into anything. Jai and I stood in the doorway, but Ennike entered in wonder while the Rose picked rags and jars out of a little chest in the farthest corner.

"We do not have to polish everything, do not worry," she said with a little chuckle. "Only the things we need for the summer rites, like the Blood rites. We need the incense-burners, combs, three ceremonial bowls, three silver candlesticks . . . I will find everything for you."

While she was speaking the shadows in the room started to draw together and flock around me. The darkness was closing in, throbbing with potency. I braced myself and raised my hands to fend off the Crone, fend off death. I was not ready! I wanted to scream but no sound came out.

The Rose stiffened and turned around. She looked at Ennike, saw what she had done, and dropped a jar of polish on the ground. The clang of metal against marble scattered the shadows and the Crone disappeared. My legs gave way at her sudden departure and I sat down on the nearest chest. Jai was the only one who noticed something was wrong with me, and she came and stood by my side. She did not touch me, but her closeness was calming.

Ennike stood next to one of the tables with a guilty look on her face. She was holding two large combs of tarnished green copper, and all the other objects the Rose had been looking for—incense-burners, bowls, candlesticks—were somehow laid out on the table in front of her.

"I only wanted to help," she said apologetically. "Forgive me, Sister, I did not know it was wrong."

"How did you know where everything was?" The Rose came over to examine the objects on the table. She picked up one of the bowls and ran her fingers around it as if to check it was real.

Ennike looked around, confused. "I—I just knew. When you named the objects I sort of saw where they were. My hands found them by themselves."

A beaming smile spread across the Rose's face and I saw tears glitter in her eyes.

"At last! I knew the Maiden would show me, but I did not know how!" She shook her head and her hair shone in the sunlight. "The First Mother does have a sense of humor."

127

We all looked at her questioningly and she laughed at our confusion. "The Maiden is the Rose, my mistress. The first aspect of the First Mother. Yet she chose to show me my novice through cleaning, a task that actually belongs to the second aspect, the Mother Havva. I would have thought the third aspect also had to be present during a choice like this."

"Novice!" said Ennike, shocked. "Me?"

"You." The Rose smiled warmly as she walked over and gently took the combs away from her. She took hold of her hands. "You shall be novice to the Rose. Can you not feel it yourself?" The Rose let go of Ennike's hands and at once became very serious. "Where is the bell we ring during the Blood rites?"

Without hesitation Ennike pointed at a little box on top of one of the lower cupboards.

"When is the Maiden at her strongest?"

"In spring at the awakening of the Spring Star." I could have given the same answer; it is what Sister O taught us. But then Ennike surprised me. "She is also strongest at the

Winter Solstice, when the Mother sleeps. She is strongest when a child is born, when the earth is plowed, and when a girl gets her first moon blood."

The Rose nodded. "How many secrets does the Maiden hold?"

"Nine."

"Whisper to me her secret name."

Ennike leaned forward with an expression of wonder on her face and whispered something in the Rose's ear. The Rose smiled and clasped Ennike's hands again.

"Do you still doubt it?"

Ennike shook her head and swallowed. "But the servant to the Rose has to be beautiful." Her voice was very meek. "That is the way it has always been. I am . . . I am covered in scars."

"The Maiden has also felt pain and fear, Ennike my daughter," the Rose said softly. "It does not make her any less beautiful."

When the light from the north window illuminated their faces so close to each other, I saw that they in fact look very similar, woman and girl. The same thick, curly hair, the same warm eyes. But more than that: their faces wear the same expression.

"You are beautiful, Ennike," I said. "And you will grow even more beautiful before the first frost comes."

I did not know why I said that. The Rose gave me a sharp look. Then she smiled softly, but with a sad look in her eyes.

"So you are here after all, Crone."

It was the day after the Rose had chosen Ennike as her novice, in the early morning when the light is still thin and shadows linger around the mountains and houses, that we were woken by the sound of the Blood bell. We got out of bed in a daze. I chased all the junior novices outside in their nightgowns and with uncovered hair. We were met in the central courtyard by stern-faced sisters in nightgowns rushing across the courtyard from Eve Steps to Dawn Steps. They grabbed hold of the novices by their hands and arms and shoulders and dragged us along with them, pushing, shoving, pulling. We sped barefoot over the cold cobblestones up toward the stairs. The Blood bell clanged incessantly between the houses and I wondered who was ringing it.

As we climbed higher a brisk morning wind swept in from the sea, lifting our nightgowns, tangling our hair. The sky was pale blue and cloudless. I heard a shout, saw a raised arm, a pointing finger. I turned to look at the sea.

A ship came sailing near the Teeth. Its white sails swelled with wind and the pointed bow plowed through the water, making mighty splashes against the sides of the vessel.

The Blood bell quietened.

I already knew. I knew who it was and I turned to look for Jai in the crowd of white-clad figures jostling their way up the steps. I had to find her before she saw the ship. I caught sight of her blond hair as she came running up with Joem and Dori.

"Jai!" I called. "Jai!"

I do not know if she heard, because at that moment Joem caught sight of the ship and pointed. As Jai looked she stopped in her tracks.

"We are lost." Her voice was weak, but I heard every word. "We are all lost!"

She began to sway.

"She is falling! Catch her!"

Sister O managed to catch Jai in her sinewy arms just as she fell. Without stopping, she swept the girl up and continued up the steps with long, deer-like strides. For a while it was chaos, no one knew what to do, everybody stared out to sea with frightened murmurs.

"Hurry!" Mother called. We all looked up and saw her standing there on the highest step, bareheaded like everyone else, her long gray hair like a silver waterfall around her shoulders. "We do not have much time."

Everybody set off at once, climbing the steps in haste, into Hearth House where Sister Ers was holding the doors open. I ran in at the same time as Mother.

"I think I have everything," I heard Sister Ers say quietly to Mother as we passed. "Some are old, how was I to know . . ."

Mother gave her a quick pat on the shoulder and continued into the hall.

I saw Joem rush past everyone and fall to her knees by the Hearth, where she quickly brought the embers to life. We positioned ourselves around the table, alternating sisters and novices. Someone went and opened all the windows wide. I stood where I could keep my eye on the Teeth and soon I saw the ship emerge from behind the farthest rock. I could not tear my eyes away from the white, foaming water.

The sun was beginning to rise on the other side of the mountains, and, as the world lit up with its first rays, I saw something gleam on the ship.

Exposed weapons.

I had never been inside Hearth House with the sisters before. Sister Mareane was standing next to me, but then she moved to make space as Sister O herded Jai in next to me and rushed away. Jai had come to her senses but was still so pale I feared she might faint again. She was not shaking. She was completely still, like a mouse face to face with a hungry cat, hoping against hope that the cat will lose interest and leave it alone.

Sister Ers, Joem, and Cissil rushed in carrying a brass dish. The dish was laid with dark-green leaves, almonds, and candied rose petals.

"Take and eat," they said as they negotiated their way between tables and shoulders. "One of each. Take. Eat. Hurry."

I reached to take some for myself but Jai did not move a muscle so I took some for her also. I helped her put an almond to her lips and ate one myself. It tasted like earth and salt. The candied rose petal was sour and sweet at the same time.

Mother walked past, calm and dignified, her hair flowing in the breeze from the open windows. In her hands she held a golden chalice.

"Eat, my daughters. Then when you have eaten, drink," said Mother. "Then when you have drunk, tame your hair. Plait and braid, weave and bind. Do not let a single strand escape."

I poked one of the strange leaves between Jai's passive lips, then stuck one in my own mouth and chewed. The bitter taste filled me, from mouth to breast, from womb to sole. It tasted of sorrow and moonlight.

A draft came scurrying across the floor and chilled my ankles. I stopped chewing.

The breath of the Crone. Her realm was close again. A hush fell around me; the only sounds were the wind and the women's quiet chewing. Was that the voice of the Crone I could hear whispering in the sails of the approaching ship? Was she saying my name? I could not swallow the leaf in my mouth. I could not move. If I moved she would find me.

Mother had come round to us and held the chalice in front of my mouth. The red wine washed down the leaf and the fear. The thick wine was sweet like honey and salty like blood.

Everyone around me had their hands in their hair, twisting, braiding, and binding with skilled, nimble fingers. Sister Loeni and Sister Nummel rushed between the benches and tables to hand out bands to tie it up with. I did not want to stand still and braid. Now that the wine had dispelled my paralysis, all I wanted to do was run. Run away from the ship, from the Crone, run up into the mountains and hide. My hands trembled as I started to braid.

The movement of my fingers through my hair calmed me. I had not braided my own hair since I lived at home, but my hands remembered how to do it. They twisted and lifted and tightened and twisted again. A calmness flowed through my body and I grew still and strong.

The wind coming through the windows began to settle.

Sister Mareane and I helped to bind Jai's hair. As the plaits formed I could feel her relax, if only a little bit. It was a calm one could not resist.

Jai was the last one to have her hair bound. When we finished the wind died down completely. Everyone stood and looked out of the window and I strained to get a better view.

The sea was still and shining like a mirror. The surface was completely calm, without the slightest ripple. The sun had risen over the horizon but was still behind the mountains. The Abbey buildings cast long, sharp shadows. The ship lay between the Teeth and the harbor with slack sails and water no longer frothed around the bow. My heart did a little leap of joy in my chest. All the sisters and novices were holding their breath.

Then there were movements on the ship. I could just about make out fair-haired men in black clothes. The shining weapons disappeared. Long contraptions came sliding out from holes along the sides of the ship.

Oars.

"To the Temple of the Rose," cried Mother in a piercing voice. "Quick."

We rushed out of Hearth House without a word. Braids whipped soft cheeks, bare feet drummed on smooth stone.

We ran. I held Jai's hand tightly in mine. Down Dawn Steps, over the central courtyard and up Eve Steps. We could see the ship the whole time. Edging ever closer. It was coming more slowly than before, but it was coming.

The Rose threw open the Temple doors and we hurried in. The colored glass did not let much of the sparse morning light into the Temple and it was almost completely dark inside. I saw two figures dressed in white move swiftly up the stairs to the platform and disappear behind the double rosewood doors. Ennike and the Rose.

We stood in the colonnade and waited.

We could not see the sea from there. We did not know where the ship was. Jai was still holding on tightly to my hand. I was terrified. I thought about what the men would do to Jai—to all of us. I thought about the outer wall and whether it was high enough. How long could it keep the men out? My mouth could still taste the bitterness of the leaf, the sweetness of the rose petal, the earthiness of the almond.

The Rose and Ennike appeared up on the platform. It was strange to see them without their hair flowing over their shoulders. They held out two long silver candlesticks and lit two fat blood-red candles. The flames did little to illuminate the Temple, but they made shadows dance in the pale dawn light. The Rose and Ennike disappeared through the doors and came out again bearing something shiny in their hands.

"Let down your hair!" screamed the Rose in a new voice, a voice that cut through the silence like a knife. Ennike echoed. "Let down your hair!" Ennike's voice was not her own either and it pierced me like a sword.

Now I could see what they were holding. It was the copper combs we had seen the day before.

We started to undo all the braids: fair and dark, red and silver.

A gust of wind swept in through the open doors.

Up on the platform the Rose and her novice loosened their hair with quick, expert movements. Then they picked up their combs and stuck them deep into their flowing hair.

A strong wind lashed at the Temple and made the rose windows rattle. The Rose let out a triumphant howl and pulled the comb through her hair with a long stroke.

"Awake, wind!" she called. "Come, storm!"

She flung her comb across the hall. I saw Sister O catch it and pull it through her hair. Another angry wind thrashed the roof of the Temple.

I undid my final braid. Small sparks flew from my hair when it was finally released. I quickly loosened Jai's braids. Her hair crackled and hissed. Combs were flying across the hall and diving into hair, making it spark and fly. The Rose and Ennike pulled their fingers through their curls and tossed their heads with loud, shrill laughter. A comb landed in my hand and I pulled it through Jai's hair first and then through mine.

The wind howled and battered furiously against the walls, ceiling, and windows, until the great marble doors flung open and crashed against the wall. The Temple was full of white-clad women stomping, swaying, and writhing, and the faster we whipped our hair, the more the wind howled. I let go of Jai and fought my way toward the door. I had to see, I had to know.

I barely recognized the world outside.

The sky was black with storm clouds. All light had

disappeared. The air was full of leaves, branches, and detritus whipped up in the angry wind. I could not see the Abbey bay from the door because Sister House was in the way, so I fought against the wind and made my way across the Temple Yard. The storm ripped and tore through my hair, and as it did so it seemed to grow more powerful still. My hair thrashed my face and eyes, blinding me. The flicks stung like whips from a thin leather strap.

It took a while to reach Eve Steps and get a clear view of the ocean. When I eventually caught sight of it, it was unlike anything I had ever seen before.

Waves higher than the Temple itself crashed against the shore. Water and foam filled the air. If the Abbey had been lower down by the beach we would have been destroyed a long time ago. The pier and the little storehouse next to it were washed away. The ocean was wiping out everything in its path.

There was no trace of the ship.

ᚹ

It took all day for the storm to die down. We waited out

the worst of it inside the Temple, then took shelter in Sister House, where the sisters tucked the youngest novices up in their own beds and the rest of us sat by the windows and watched as the ocean reshaped the entire coastline.

As evening drew near, it finally became calm enough for us to risk going outside and down Eve Steps. Sister Ers and her novices rushed off to prepare the evening meal, while Sister Kotke took the rest of the novices to Body's Spring. The hot water was deeply soothing and we were allowed to stay in the bathing pool for as long as we wanted. Instead of going into the cold bath afterward, we got dressed in the clothes that Sister Nummel brought us from Novice House. All the other sisters had hastened to see what damage had been done by the storm, and probably also to perform rituals and ceremonies I knew nothing about. Ennike was not with us. She had stayed in the Temple with the Rose.

Jai was unresponsive through it all. She did not speak and only moved if I pushed or pulled her along with me. I had to dry her hair and help her get dressed. As I was pulling her toward Dawn Steps on our way to Hearth House to eat, she stopped in the middle of the central courtyard and looked in the direction of the sea. We could not actually see it over the wall from where we stood, but we could hear the surf sputter and hiss against the rocks on the beach. The wind was still brisk and cold.

"They are still here," she whispered. I had to lean forward to hear her words before the wind snapped them up. "I can feel it. They are out there somewhere. He'll never give up, Maresi. Honor and pride are all he has. Without them he is nothing. He will do anything to get me back, and to punish me."

She did not cry. She did not scream. But her resignation worried me more than her fear.

"But do you not see that the Abbey protects you?" I said softly. "You did not come to harm today and you never will."

She turned and looked at me for the first time since she had seen the ship.

"He will *not* give up. He will be back."

We spent the whole of the next day clearing up after the storm. Dislodged roof tiles needed to be replaced, the yards were full of rubbish, and a tree had fallen across the mountain path and had to be sawed up and transported away. Large chunks of rock had tumbled down the mountainsides and ripped away a part of the wall where the drop to the sea is at its steepest. Sister Nar walked around grumbling about all the destruction to Knowledge Garden, and even Sister Mareane's usually smooth forehead was wrinkled with deep worry lines. Even our orchards had been damaged by the storm.

Jai, Ennike, and I were assigned to help Sister Veerk and Luan clean up the beach. We found some remains of the pier and storehouse—the rest had been swept away by the sea. Sister Veerk made diligent notes about everything we needed to replace. Soon our arms and backs ached from hauling heavy wet logs and planks farther up the beach, safe from the ocean's ravenous waves. There was still a strong wind blowing that made our hair dance before our eyes and stick in the corners of our mouths when we spoke. I looked at Jai's fair hair, at Ennike's and Luan's brown hair, and at Sister Veerk's stringy black hair, all flowing free under their headscarves. So much hidden power.

Ennike and I were dragging a dark, age-cracked log out of the water. I looked over at Jai who was standing up to her middle in the cold sea next to Sister Veerk and Luan, heaving up stones that had rolled down and blocked the harbor. She groaned and screwed up her face with the strain. When a large rock required particular effort she roared loudly. Then she rested her hands on the rock, bowed her head, and panted for a brief moment before poking Luan in the side to continue with the next stone together. Sister Veerk said something to her that I could not hear. I saw Jai hiss an answer.

Jai had not retreated into her shell this time. She had gotten angry.

We walked together up the narrow staircase to the

Abbey. I showed her some pieces of smooth gray driftwood I had collected from the beach. She scowled at them and turned away from me.

"Nobody is listening," she said and started up the steps with long, angry stomps. "Everyone is running around worrying about the pier and the *fruit trees*." She spat out the words. "And you!" She turned around so fast I bumped into her. Her hair was flailing in the wind and her eyes were black. I took a step back. "You know. No one else knows except you and Mother and probably a couple of the sisters. You know what happened to Unai. You know what Father wants. Do you think anyone will be spared when he really comes for us? Do you think he will be satisfied with taking only me? He will have his revenge on everyone who sheltered me. Everyone. And you go around collecting *driftwood*."

She spun around and marched up the steps without looking back. I stayed where I was and swallowed hard. What did she want from me? If she had asked me to do something, I would have done it without question. But I did not know how I could help her if she insisted on blaming me.

ω

We did nothing but clean up all that day and all the next. There were no lessons and we ate in Hearth House whenever we had time between tasks. Jai did not talk to me. She avoided me. She was acting differently, sharp and prickly like a thistle, and I did not know how to react to her snorts and scowls. She made sure we did not have the same duties, and on the second day I barely saw her at all. At first my heart ached for her. She was scared and I understood that. But why was she only angry with me? She had no reason to punish me!

I spent all afternoon carrying freshly sawn wood from the mountain path down to the woodshed by Hearth House. When evening came my hands were shaking from the strain, my arms ached and I barely made it to Hearth House to get some food.

Jai sat at one of the long tables talking to Cissil and Joem. I know she saw me but she avoided eye contact. They sat huddled together in an intense private conversation.

I took a cup of water and filled my plate with bread, cheese, and pickled onion from the serving table. I looked over at Jai and realized I did not know where to sit. She was still acting as if I did not exist. I walked slowly past her and sat a little farther away at the same table. None of them looked at me or let me join in the conversation. I stared out of the window on the west wall and tried to act as if I had chosen to sit alone, chewing on my bread as quickly as I could. I did not want Jai or Joem to see that I was upset.

When I had finished eating I got up and tried to catch Jai's eye. She turned toward Joem and said something that made her nod emphatically. I stared straight ahead as I walked out of Hearth House with my lips pressed tightly together. I had been fine without Jai before she came to the Abbey, so I could be fine without her again.

That evening I had to go to the treasure chamber alone and that evening I wished for company more than ever. Sister O was not in her room when I knocked but she had given me permission to take the key in her absence, so I lifted it down and took it across the Temple Yard to Knowledge House in the fading evening light. Fear gripped me as soon as I opened the door. I wished I had Jai by my side.

I walked stiffly down the corridor. I was approaching the door to the crypt. It was the first time I had had to walk past it alone since the Crone spoke to me. I clutched the key hard, as some sort of protection, as a dagger. As I neared the door I started to run, quickly and quietly and though I did not hear the Crone, I knew she was there behind it. Biding her time.

When the doors to the treasure chamber were shut behind me I finally felt safe. I inhaled the familiar smell of dust and parchments. I stood awhile and just breathed. It was so different being there without Jai. It was like before she came, and yet it was not: I was used to her company now. Used to discussing which books we would choose, hearing her turn pages, and then talking over what we had read while we locked the door to the treasure chamber and walked out through the dusky, dark house.

That evening I chose the ancient tales of the First Sisters. I have always loved reading about their journey to the island, their struggle to build Knowledge House, and their survival in the first few years with nothing but fish and foraged wild fruits and berries as sustenance. Life on the island was difficult for the first few years. It did not get easier until some decades later, when they discovered the bloodsnail colony and the silver began to flow in.

I love reading about the island's first novice, and how rumors started to spread and the Abbey became a sanctuary for the vulnerable and the persecuted. I reveled in the story and the comforting sense of security it always afforded me.

It was already late in the evening and the light from the window was gray and dim. The massive bookshelves loomed in silence along the walls, full of treasure. The First Sisters planned all of this. They knew they would preserve their knowledge for generations of women after them. How must it have felt when they found the island and were saved? What were they thinking about?

Amid the prevailing silence, I heard the door to Knowledge House open and shut. Rapid footsteps came along the long corridor and the library doors were thrown open.

"There you are. Sister O said I would find you here." Sister Loeni stood in the door with her hands on her hips. "I know it is late and you have been working hard, but Sister

Ers has just discovered that a fallen tree made a hole in the storehouse roof. We must mend it immediately, at least temporarily; else the food store will be ruined if it rains. You have been assigned to help."

"I am so tired," I said quietly. It was true. As I put the books back in their places under Sister Loeni's watchful eyes, my arms were trembling so much I had to struggle with the heavier volumes. She tutted disapprovingly and shook her head.

"If I was responsible for the library I would never let you run around doing whatever you please. Sister O gives you too much freedom, so she does. She shouldn't give you such preferential treatment."

She does not show me preferential treatment at all, I thought, but out loud I simply said, "Is there no one else who can help?"

I locked the door behind me begrudgingly and gave the key to Sister Loeni, who was standing with her hand outstretched expectantly.

"There are several of us already working on it, Maresi. Everyone else is busy with other things. Now then, do not dally. It will not take long and then you can go to bed. No more reading for today."

But it did take a long time to clear away the tree and mend the roof. By the time we finished it was already night. My head was aching with fatigue but my body was jittering with worry. Something stopped me from going to Novice House and to bed. I felt I needed to see the horizon and be able to breathe solitude. When the sisters were not looking I stole away into the shadows, left through the goat door, and walked up the mountainside.

I know the mountain above the Abbey as well as I know Knowledge House, but this time everything was different. Stones had rolled down the slope and there were fallen trees and branches everywhere. I could not see the path in the faint twilight and I soon went astray. Suddenly I found myself too far north, looking down on the Temple of the Rose. I sat down on a rock and tightened my pullover around my shoulders. The night's first stars were shining in the west. The sea glittered silver under the crescent of the new moon, caressed by a cool night wind. The Abbey rested in darkness below me. Everybody was asleep. The only lamplight came from Moon House and from Sister O's window. Beneath me the island of Menos mumbled and sighed, getting ready for sleep. Even the nightbirds had settled down to rest. The stillness, the beauty, and the crescent moon calmed my senses, but my anxiety refused to let go completely. I thought about Jai, who had been my friend since her very first day but had now turned away from me. I could not understand why.

After a while my toes felt stiff with cold and I realized it was time to go back. I got up and started walking tentatively in the direction of where I thought the path should be. The slope was slippery with fallen leaves and naked earth. I stumbled several times and was not entirely sure where I was. Some bushes appeared in front of me that I could not remember seeing before.

Suddenly I stepped on something soft. The ground beneath me gave way and a hole opened under my feet. I managed to lurch forward in time so I did not fall down the hole but hung there instead with my belly on the ground and legs dangling down. The storm must have uncovered an underground cavern.

I heard a rustling around me. In the faint moonlight I saw hundreds of iridescent butterflies flutter up out of the bushes. Their wings looked unnaturally large and they shone silver and gray in the soft light. The butterflies seemed never-ending as more and more and more flew out of the bushes and into the night. I was entranced by the beauty and stayed hanging there, enraptured. It was like a goodnight greeting from the island itself.

When the last butterfly had flown I heard the voice.

Maresi, it whispered. *My daughter.*

It came from the hole beneath me. She was there in the darkness. Waiting. I could feel her icy grasp on my feet. She was grappling to get hold of me. I kicked and screamed as loud as I could to drown out the sound of her voice.

"You cannot have me!" I screamed. "I am not yours!"

I crawled up and out of the Crone's icy reach. The bushes around me were still rustling. At first I thought it was more butterflies, but this time skinny shapes came slithering out through the grass and around my feet. Snakes. Dozens, hundreds of snakes wriggled hissing from the bush. They disappeared into holes, under stones, between knotted cypress roots. I stood dead still. Snakes are rarely seen on the island, and here were more snakes than I had ever seen before in my whole life. They made me think of the handle on the Crone's door, and fear seized me in its strong grip. I wanted to run away from the cavern and the Crone but I could not move for fear of the snakes. Only when the last snake had disappeared did I dare take a single step. Then a second step. I stamped every step as hard as I could in my sandals to frighten away the snakes.

To frighten away the Crone herself, if I could.

It took me an eternity to get back to the path. When I finally found it in the darkness I ran down to the goat door. I had left it ajar and now I closed it behind me.

I closed it, I know I did. I can still hear the click from when I pulled it shut behind me. But I cannot remember if I bolted it.

I was so tired and so afraid of the Crone. I wanted to go to my bed, to safety under my own blanket. My legs were shaking and my arms were aching after the day's work. I usually always bolt the door, but however much I think about it, I cannot remember if I did that night.

I crept into bed. For a short while I lay there listening to the other girls breathing. I knew that if I stretched my hand out to Jai she would not take it. Finally I was so exhausted that sleep took hold of me and enveloped me like a grave. I slept so deeply and dreamlessly that it took me a long time to swim back up to the surface when a rhythmic noise cut into my sleep.

It was long before dawn. The sound that woke me came from the window. A sharp, rhythmic tapping.

In the bed next to mine Jai sat upright, her hands twitching and gripping the edge of her blanket. She was staring at the window.

There was a flapping and rustling outside. Something large thudded against the glass. Then the tapping started again, this time even more insistent.

Dori's Bird made a whistling sound. Dori jumped up out of bed, rushed over to the window and flung it open before I could stop her.

In flew a koan bird, the symbol of the Abbey. It circled the dormitory and let out a single piercing shriek. Dazed heads and groans of protest emerged from the beds around me. Jai did not take her eyes off the koan bird.

"The birds . . ." she said quietly. "The birds bring warning."

Ennike had woken up. She was listening but did not say a word.

Dori's Bird chattered indignantly.

"It is breeding season," said Dori. "The koan birds are breeding on the other side of the mountain." We exchanged a glance.

"There are sheltered coves in the east," I said slowly.

"They have come," whispered Jai.

"They do not know the mountains. It will take them a long time to find their way here. And it is dark." Dori called to the koan bird with a whistle and it came to her at once. She stroked its feathers while Bird looked on jealously, then she carefully shooed the koan bird out and shut the window. I sat up and swung my legs over the edge of the bed.

As soon as my feet touched the floor I could feel her. The Crone was very close. I could feel her hunger and her darkness. The door to her realm was still closed, but the Crone's pungent breath came floating through the night.

I took a deep breath.

"They are close. Maybe already over the mountain."

We looked at one another. Jai, Dori, Ennike and I. We racked our brains in quiet desperation, thinking what we should do.

Jai threw her blanket aside. "I am waking Sister Nummel."

"I will run to Mother," said Dori, and they were both out of the door in a flash. Ennike ran around and shook the still-sleeping novices awake.

I sat down. The ship and the men did not concern me. It was not them I feared. It was the thought of the Crone's voice that froze up my limbs. I could not move. My heart was thudding wildly. My arms felt the weight of Anner's body again. I had tried to protect her and give her some of my food, but she was already a weak child when she was born. Sickly. I could not get her to eat. I could not get her fever down. She could not withstand the Crone's siren call. She left me with empty arms.

I was still sitting there when Sister Nummel entered the room.

"How can you be so sure?" she said to Jai, who came in after her. "A single bird is not a sign." She looked at the frightened faces of the half-asleep novices.

"Honestly, Maresi." Sister Nummel glared at me. "They listen to you, that is not a power you should abuse. Think of the junior novices. They will be scared out of their minds."

The junior novices. They had to get out of bed. The thought of them shot life into my paralyzed limbs. I quickly put on my pullover, stuck my left foot in a sandal and made my way between the beds, hopping on one leg to get the other sandal on. Sister Nummel protested but I did not hear what she said. Jai looked at me and gave me a quick nod. She ripped the blanket away from the novice nearest to her.

"Up, at once! Get dressed. Warm clothes over your nightgowns. Now."

I rushed past Ennike's bed and into the junior novices' dormitory. I stood in the doorway and looked at the sleeping heads on white sheets. Thin little necks and half-open mouths. Heo, Ismi, Leitha, Sirna and Paene. Jai's words echoed in my head. *He will have his revenge on everyone who sheltered me. Everyone.* I could feel the Crone. She was pulling us toward her door.

"Up, girls," I whispered so as not to scare them. "You must get up at once. Get dressed."

They were all so used to doing what I said that they sat up and stretched their arms to be dressed. The sleepiness in their eyes and mouths prevented them from asking questions. I herded them into the other dormitory, where Sister Nummel stood with arms crossed angrily over her chest. The older novices stood in a scared huddle looking at me and Sister Nummel and not knowing whom to believe. When Ismi saw them she burst into tears and Heo put a skinny little arm around her shoulders.

"Do not cry, Ismi. Maresi is here. She can protect us." Heo's voice was calm and full of trust.

I had almost betrayed them. My fear cost us a lot of precious time.

Jai came running and I left the junior novices for a moment to follow her into the yard. I heard Sister Nummel come after us. The thin crescent of the new moon hung low in the sky. Goddess help us, her power is at its weakest now, I thought. Not much was visible in the sparse light. The central courtyard was empty. The night lay thick over the island. Sister Nummel stood behind me and took a deep breath in preparation to tell us off.

Up by Hearth House we heard a scream. We could all recognize Cissil's voice. Then a metallic clang. The slam of a door. Another scream. Silence.

"The goat door," whispered Sister Nummel. "They have come through the goat door."

"Hearth House." I could barely get the words out. That is where Cissil, Joem, and Sister Ers slept.

Two figures came hurrying down Moon Steps followed by a dark, flapping shape. Mother, Dori, and Bird.

"Up to the Temple Yard," Mother called without stopping. "They have surrounded us. I saw them from the Moon Yard. Some are waiting outside the main gate in case we try to escape. But they cannot have got through there. They must have come through the goat door."

Jai and I were back into Novice House before she had even finished her sentence.

"Get out. The men are here. Up to the Temple Yard this instant."

I picked up Leitha, the littlest one, took Heo by the hand, and ran. Jai came after me leading Ismi and Paene by the hand, and I saw Ennike pulling Sirna along with her. I

161

could hear the sound of running feet behind me as all the other novices followed behind. Sister Nummel was waiting for us outside, counting us as we ran past.

Eve Steps had never felt so long. Leitha gripped my neck so tightly I almost choked. I had to slow down so that Heo could keep up. I could barely see where to put my feet in the darkness and I stumbled many times, hitting my shins and stubbing my toes.

At last we got to the top. Mother and all the sisters were gathered in the Temple Yard.

"I cannot allow that," I heard Mother whisper to the Rose as I stopped beside them. "Never."

"They are going to do it anyway," said the Rose. She looked very rigid and pale. "You know it. This way at least I can protect the others." Her eyes ran over me and the other novices behind me and back to Mother's face. "The little ones."

"Eostre," Mother said, her voice barely a whisper.

"I am not Eostre any more. I am servant to the Rose, I am the Maiden incarnate. This is my domain."

"We have to block the stairs," said Sister O brusquely. "Now. They are already down in the central courtyard, can you not hear them? They are searching Novice House and Body's Spring."

"That is impossible," said Sister Loeni. "We will never make it in time."

"We have to try." Mother turned to me. "Maresi, remember what I asked you. Take the children to Knowledge House. Take them down into the crypt. It is the safest place on the island. We can only hope they do not realize too soon that it is a door. Barricade it from the inside if you can. And take Jai. Goddess be with you." Mother looked sternly at the other older novices. "Do you want to go with Maresi and Jai?"

I hoisted Leitha farther up on my hip. "Come! Hurry up!" I could hear aggressive shouts and vulgar laughter coming from down in the central courtyard and started edging back toward Knowledge House.

Ennike shook her head. "Not me. If no one of Jai's age stays here they will be suspicious. They will search for you. But if some of us stay here maybe we can fool them."

"I will stay too," said Dori. Toulan nodded without a word.

I could not wait any longer. Once I had opened the doors to Knowledge House and ushered in the little ones I glanced over my shoulder. The sisters were in the Temple Yard facing the steps, forming a wall in front of the novices. Mother stood at the front with arms raised high.

None of the novices came with us.

J ai and I locked the door behind us and hurried into Knowledge House with the little ones in our arms and holding our hands. We stopped at the door to the crypt. The only way to distinguish the door from the rest of the corridor is by the writing, which was difficult to make out in the dim light.

"How do you open it?" Jai whispered.

"I have never been inside," I answered quietly. Standing so close to the realm of the Crone was making me feel dizzy. "But Sister O said that all you have to do is know it is a door."

I put my hand over the writing and pressed. Without a sound, a large section of stone slid inward and revealed a staircase leading down into pitch-darkness. An ice-cold draft made the little girls shiver. Otherwise they were very calm. Maybe they did not entirely understand what was happening. They did not cry or complain. But I could feel the Crone's breath and I gulped.

"Are we going down there?" asked Heo.

"Yes, but we need light," I answered. "Otherwise we could fall and hurt ourselves. Jai, take the girls inside while I fetch lamps. If you hear anything shut the door behind you immediately."

Jai ushered the girls in through the doorway and I ran down the corridor to the classroom where we keep lamps and tinderboxes for our occasional evening lessons. As, with shaking hands, I picked up two oil lamps, I heard a sound coming from the yard that I had not heard for years.

The sound of a man's voice.

I had to know what was happening. I put the lamps down on the table quietly and crept over to the window.

The men had come up Eve Steps. I could not see their faces properly in the light of the thin crescent moon. They were like a dense mass of darkness in front of Mother, who stood with raised arms and her gray hair loose down her back. The sisters stood behind her, and behind them were the novices, shivering in their nightgowns like petals on apple flowers. The men were an undulating mass of barely restrained violence, ready at any moment to rip the petals apart and throw them into the sea, dash them against the rocks, spear them on their sharp weapons that glinted in the moonlight. I saw wild blond beards, shaved heads, hands tattooed with peculiar symbols.

Mother had no defense against attack, only her outstretched hands.

"Men are forbidden on this island." Her voice was so clear and sharp that it cut through the rattle of steel and angry voices, through the windowpanes separating me from the yard.

"Men are forbidden in this Abbey." Her voice did not falter. It was as clear as the clang of the Blood bell. "Leave at once. Go back to your ship. Sail away and you will live as long as your life thread allots to you."

I could see Mother's profile. She looked resolute and authoritative. Her voice made the men hesitate. It stopped them drawing their daggers and advancing. They remembered the eerie lull before the sudden storm. They backed up.

Then one man pushed past the others. He had fair clipped hair and a well-trimmed beard. I could not distinguish the color of his clothes but his jacket had a richly embroidered collar and his dagger had a decorated shaft. I knew who he was at once.

Jai's father.

"Where is she? Where is that little whore?"

When he came face to face with Mother and all her strength and solemnity, he hesitated but did not retreat. He tightened his grip on the shaft of his dagger.

"Give me what is mine, woman, and I will leave you unharmed and in peace."

But the look in his eyes told a different story.

"You are mistaken," said Mother calmly, her hands still held high. They did not quiver. "There is nothing of yours here. And it is you and your men who will suffer harm."

Jai's father raised his hand and knocked Mother aside, and his men gasped in fear, but nothing happened.

"Stop whimpering like dogs," he roared. He leaned in towards Mother. "Where is she? Where is my—" he spat out the word "—daughter?"

"She is my daughter now," Mother answered calmly. "Leave."

"Quiet!" bellowed Jai's father and turned to his men. "Search the buildings. Okret, take one group. Vinjan, take some men with you. You know who you are looking for."

The men drew their daggers. A few came and surrounded the sisters and novices. One of them, who seemed to be the leader, stood very close to Sister O and the Rose. He was wearing a jacket that shone like silk in the moonlight and he had a two-pronged beard that was so blond it was almost white. A saw-toothed dagger as long as my forearm hung from his belt. He had many tattoos on his hands and forehead. He stared hard at the Rose. The Rose was turned toward the ocean and staring out with unseeing eyes.

The other men were led away by two men in similar clothes to Jai's father, one old, one young. They soon returned.

"The houses are empty, Brother," said the older man and stood next to Jai's father. "Nobody is there."

"But that house is locked, Uncle," said the younger man, pointing at Knowledge House. He wore a black jacket like Jai's father. He did not look up at his uncle; instead he looked over to the sisters, then down at the ground, and ran his fingers nervously over the dagger in his belt.

169

"So go and get something to break down the door!" roared Jai's father. "Now!"

I jumped down from the windowsill and snatched the lamps and tinderboxes.

I kicked off my sandals and ran silently through the corridor back to the crypt. I could hear the sound of men's voices outside the door, more muffled than before. I could not make out the words. They would soon find something to break down the door. Very soon.

When I joined the others, Jai had already heard the men's voices and did not waste a second in closing the door behind me. It shut without a sound. Only then did I dare light the oil lamps. Pale faces met me in the low light. The flickering flames lit up gray stone walls and a winding staircase. We dared not speak; we just went down one by one in silence. I had no choice but to swallow my fear and go first. The staircase was not long and when we came to the bottom I think we were about level with the central courtyard. The stairs led into a long, narrow room with a low ceiling, natural stone walls and alcoves along both sides. The room was cold and undecorated, but it was not abandoned. The floor was swept clean and a little altar was set up in the middle of the room with gifts to the Crone: a winter apple from last autumn, some beautiful moonstones, and a shed snakeskin.

Jai and I held out our lamps and took a few tentative steps inside the room. The light glowed in the alcoves. The recesses contained the remains of all the sisters who had lived and died on Menos. The Crone's shadows were hiding between the bones and in the skulls' dark eye sockets. I had never felt her presence so strongly before, not even during Moon Dance. I could not see the door to her realm, but I knew it was there, ever waiting, biding its time. The little girls kept close to me and Jai, quiet and solemn. The room was very long and the far end was in darkness.

"I cannot see anything to barricade the door with," said Jai, lifting the lamp. I swallowed and shook my head.

"We can only hope they do not find it."

When we reached the far end of the room we saw that it was not a room at all, but a natural cave, part of a whole cave system, which the sisters had chiseled and shaped into a crypt for their dead. The short side of the cave was blocked with a large wooden door, rotten with age. Next to it there were seven alcoves, which were a little bigger than the others, each laid with fresh flowers. The names of the dead were written on brass plaques. *Kabira. Clarás. Garai. Estegi. Orseola. Sulani. Daera.* After each name there was an ornate mark. Maybe an *I.*

I told the junior novices to sit down, and Jai and I put our lamps down on the ground. The girls arranged themselves in a neat little circle as if they were having a picnic on White Lady's slopes. When I sat down Heo immediately crawled into my lap.

"Will the men come down here?" asked Ismi.

"Don't be silly," answered Heo assuredly. "Maresi is here. They would not dare. And if they do try," she gave a great big yawn, "don't you remember the Moon women? They will probably come and roll boulders down on them again."

Soon they all fell asleep resting on one another, with heads on knees and arms around waists.

Jai could not keep still. She walked the length of the crypt until she disappeared in the darkness, turned around and paced back, over and over again. Her eyes were wild and her fists tightly clenched.

She saw me watching her and came up to me.

"It is my fault that the Abbey is being destroyed. You are all going to die, and I am the one who brought death here. I should never have come." She stretched a hand toward me. "Give me the key to the main door. I will go out now and surrender myself. Maybe he will spare everybody else." She smiled an unbearably hopeless little smile. "If there is anyone still out there to spare."

"You are not going." I carefully shifted Heo's head and she sighed lightly in her sleep. "Not now, not ever. Mother is taking care of us. You must have faith that she will not let anything happen."

I did not even know if I believed what I was saying. I wanted to believe it. Mother had already chased the men away once.

But this time she had failed. The men had gotten onto the island. They were in the Abbey with their shining weapons.

Jai stood in front of me with her hand still stretched out and jaws tightly clenched.

"Give me the key! I do not want your blood on my hands!"

"Shh. You will wake up the little ones. The men cannot

get in here. Do you not remember the story? We are protected in Knowledge House."

At that very moment there was a terrible crash. It came from the house above us, and the sound echoed all around the mountain.

Jai's eyes met mine.

"The main door!"

"You cannot go anywhere now or the men will discover our hiding place and find the little ones. We stay here until Mother comes and gets us."

I sounded more decisive than I felt. The chill of the door, the breath of the Crone. She was waiting. She was craving her offering. I did not even know if there was anyone left to come and get us.

Anyone who was not carrying shining weapons.

I was woken by an indistinct noise. I was sitting with my back against the cool stone wall and Heo weighing on my legs. I could not believe I had actually slept. It felt like a betrayal of everybody else outside. I was sure none of them was sleeping. If they were even still alive.

I carefully leaned forward to turn up the oil lamps, and I realized one of them was missing. So was Jai.

I gently lifted Heo off my knee. She woke up anyway and made a sleepy little noise like a kitten.

"What is it, Maresi?"

"Shh, do not wake the others. I am going to see where Jai has gone."

"She is probably exploring the caves," said Heo in a muffled voice. She curled up with her head on Ismi's feet. "I saw her looking before."

At first I did not understand what she meant. But then I noticed that some of the rotten boards in the door at the end of the crypt had been broken off.

I looked around. I could not take the lamp with me because the girls would be scared in the dark. One of the dry, brittle board stumps lay on the ground.

I carefully poured a dash of oil from the lamp onto the board and held it to the flame. It caught fire immediately.

"Heo, I will be back soon," I said. She mumbled in response. I ducked through the hole Jai had made and into the darkness.

The cave was even narrower here; more like a long passage with an uneven floor that sloped gently upward. I held the board high enough that the flame would not dazzle me, though in reality it was more for a sense of security than to light my way. I ran my free hand along the wall. I could not leave the little ones alone for long. But I could not let Jai surrender herself to her father.

I thought of what Sister O had said about people's responsibility for their own lives, and the evil things they do to one another. I quickened my pace.

The flame flickered and died. I stopped still. Darkness pressed in on me from all sides. A darkness as dense as the one I knew was on the other side of the Crone's door.

Or almost as dense. Far off in the distance there was a faint glow of warm yellow light. I threw down the board and began to run toward the light, feeling my way along the walls of the passage with my hands.

I eventually found Jai standing still and looking up with her lamp raised high. "There, you see," she said when I reached her, out of breath. She pointed upward. "The night sky. There is a way out."

"You mustn't, Jai," I said when I had caught my breath. "You are one of us now. You do not belong to him anymore."

"That is why I must do it," she said and turned to me. She was incredibly calm. "Because I am one of you. Because you are as dear to me as Unai." The lamp lit her face from below and her eyes looked like inky black wells. "You have to help me up."

"Never."

We looked at each other. She was not going to give in, I could see that. But without my help she could not reach the hole in the ceiling. I looked up and saw that the sky was pale with the first hour of dawn. Some spidery branches were swaying in the light sea breeze.

177

"I know where that is," I said slowly. "It is on the mountainside just above the Temple of the Rose. I found the hole yesterday."

I had to think of a way to stop Jai surrendering to her father. She had made up her mind and nothing I said could sway her. If I did not help her out here she would go back and leave through the main door.

The Crone was murmuring in the darkness around us. Her words tasted of death. Above my head there was light, sky, and fresh sea breeze—a way to escape the Crone's door.

"I could climb up and see what is happening. Maybe they are giving up. " I looked at Jai and hoped she would not protest. "But then you have to stay with the little ones. Keep them safe and calm. They are your sisters now, Jai. I will come back soon and tell you what I saw."

Jai was quiet for a long time. The lamp's glow distorted her features and I could not read what she was thinking. At last she gave a quick nod, set down the lamp, and interlaced her fingers. I put my foot in her hands and, with arms strong from months of hard work around the Abbey, she heaved me up. I grabbed hold of a tree root and found footing in a dent in the craggy rock wall. I climbed up a little way, and clung on tight between darkness and light. I could not find any holds so I had to grope around with my hand until I found something I hoped would take my weight. I lifted myself farther up and got some purchase on the tree root. I was not far from the surface now. I could see the roots and branches that had stopped me from falling the night before. The rocky wall was not entirely vertical and I found holds for my fingers, knees, and toes, and scrambled my way up. As I reached the roots I used their hairy tangles to pull myself farther up and out into the dawn. Once I had emerged I turned around to poke my head down the hole.

"I will be back before the sun is a hand's breadth over the horizon," I whispered. "Do not do anything foolish in the meantime, Jai."

She did not answer. I could not see her face down there, only a figure in white next to the faint lamp glow. Then I heard her voice come up out of the hole, deep and husky.

"Be careful, Maresi. My sister."

The first thing I noticed was the lack of noise. No doors opening and shutting, no well winch creaking, no happy shouts from playful girls. The Abbey had never been so quiet and still. I could hear anxious bleating from the goat house where the goats were waiting for their morning milking. The sound only intensified the ear-piercing silence.

A silence much like the one that emanated from the Crone's door.

It was dawn, but the sun had not risen yet and the Abbey still lay in half-light. From my place up on the mountainside I could see the familiar shapes of the Abbey buildings below. Nearest to me was the Temple of the Rose, with its longest side against the steep face of the mountain. I could not see the Temple Yard behind it but I could see Knowledge House and Knowledge Garden to its right. The garden had been desecrated. Plants had been ripped up by the roots or stamped down into the soil. The sea

181

breeze carried the smell of the dying plants: peppery, bitter, and sweet.

The central courtyard lay in shadow to my left, and beyond that was the Hearth Yard on the slopes up to White Lady. The door to Hearth House was open.

The men were nowhere to be seen. This frightened me even more than when I could actually see them with their shining daggers and tattooed hands.

I crept down the mountain slope. At first there were some bushes and cypress trees to hide behind, but farther down there was only grass and the thick leaves of korr-root. I went as quietly as I could. There is a narrow path between the Temple of the Rose and Knowledge House that does not lead anywhere but comes to an end at the outer wall that runs close behind the houses. The outer wall is not high there—nobody imagined intruders could get over the mountain and attack from the northeast—but it was still too high for me to get over. Dori's Bird was perched on top of it.

Its blue tail feathers looked black in the pale dawn light. It flitted nervously about and looked down at the Temple Yard. I stopped just below it.

"Bird," I said, and still today I do not know why I did this. "Bird, where is Dori?"

Bird turned around and peered down at me. Its dark eyes were shining.

Then it let out a short squawk and flew down onto my head. Its sharp claws scratched my scalp and tangled my hair. I tried to lift it off but then another pair of claws gripped me by the forearm. My hair had fallen forward, so I could not see what kind of bird it was. As I carefully tried to shake it off, yet another bird landed on my shoulder, then the other shoulder, then on my hands. I was gripped by pair after pair of claws, which, though sharp, did not harm me. I lost count of how many birds there were and I stood totally still under the weight of them all until suddenly the weight disappeared. I was flying. In a flash, the birds lifted me and let me down again, then silently flew away. At that point I could not even be sure there ever were any birds. All I knew was that, when Bird jumped down from my head onto my right hand and I brushed the hair out of my face with my left, I found myself on the other side of the outer wall. From there I could follow the path between Knowledge House and the Temple of the Rose into the Temple Yard. I saw shadowy movements. Then I could hear voices—coarse, dark voices that did not belong here.

I hurried up to Knowledge House and pressed myself against its wall. Bird flew away from my hand and I carefully peeked around the corner.

Bird sat on the ledge of one of the rose windows. It tapped on the glass with its long beak and cawed forlornly. A stone came flying from the yard. It missed Bird by a hair's breadth and smashed a hole through the reddish glass. Male laughter came from the yard. Bird rose in a cloud of caws and ruffled red and blue feathers, but landed again at once, even though it knew it was at risk of being aimed at again.

Dori had to be in the Temple.

The shadows of the men moved to and fro in the yard. When another stone hit a windowpane right next to Bird, it gave up and flew onto the roof ridge. I heard laughter and rough voices. One of the men came into my sight and stood with his back to me. I could see his shaved head and tree-trunk thighs. I recognized him by the dagger that glinted on his belt: long and saw-toothed. It was the one who seemed senior to the others in the crew. The one who had stood so close to the Rose. A tattooed hand clutched a large stone. The hand was missing several fingers. The man looked up to the roof where Bird was perched out of throwing distance.

"We haven't found her yet, so what makes you think we're going to?" a voice said, and the man turned to look at the speaker. "Sarjan's been listening to tall tales. She's not here. We should sail away. That storm wasn't natural, whatever Sarjan says."

The fingerless man shrugged. "So we do what we really came here to do. Then we can sail away and look somewhere else."

"Sail home you mean," snorted a third man. "I heard that little sissy Vinjan say there's masses of silver in that house up there." He pointed at the Moon Yard. "That's where we can get our payment from."

"And from in there." The fingerless man pointed at the Temple of the Rose and the men exploded into laughter.

I had to find a way to see what was happening inside the Temple.

Just behind me was the low wall that guarded Knowledge Garden. It runs at right angles to the outer wall that guards the Abbey. I climbed up and balanced on the low wall, facing the higher one. It was not difficult to climb onto the outer wall from there. It is wide and easy to walk on. There is nothing to hide behind, but I took the risk and ran along it, past the narrow path where the men could easily see me from the Temple Yard, if they happened to look in my direction at that moment. I did not hear anything so assumed they had not seen me. When I reached the back side of the Temple I was at eye level with the high window that is sunk into a deep niche in the wall. I managed to leap over into the niche. The glass is colored, so there was a chance that I could see in better than they could see me through it.

I cupped my hands around my eyes and peeked in.

When my eyes eventually adjusted to the dark I could see the whole Temple hall. Novices and sisters were cramped between the columns, quiet and still. They were facing the door with their backs to me. I tried to count to check they were all there. I thought about Cissil, Sister Ers, and Joem, who were alone up in Hearth House when the men came. It was difficult to see in the scant light and every time I counted I came to a different total. But when a novice moved by one of the columns the red light from the window lit up her copper-colored hair. It was Cissil. She was alive.

After a little while I could see the men more clearly. Two by the door and three up on the platform, playing dice.

Dice. In the Temple of the Rose.

I knew that the men had defiled the island simply by stepping ashore, but this hit me harder than anything else. Men in the Temple of the Rose. The Goddess had not managed to hold them back.

The Temple doors were heaved open. Jai's father stormed in. He was followed by the men I had seen him give orders to, the ones who had called him Uncle and Brother. Everybody had curved silver daggers shining in their belts. Jai's father's was clearly the most valuable, with red jewels on the hilt. They marched past the huddle of women and up to the platform.

"Where is she?" said Jai's father. His low voice was more menacing than his shout. "I want to talk to the leader!"

There was a jostle amongst the group of women. Mother made her way forward to the steps. Jai's father pointed at her.

"One last time. Where is my daughter?"

Mother met his gaze but did not answer. He cursed, came down the steps, and smacked Mother hard in the mouth, flinging her head back. She did not so much as take one step back. The three men who sat playing dice got to their feet immediately, expecting something to happen, but nothing did.

"There, you see?" Jai's father turned toward the dice-players. "You are afraid of them but they do not have any magic powers. It was a storm like any other storm the ship has been through, nothing to do with them. They are ordinary weak women just like back home."

Slowly, as if he were instructing a class of novices, he pulled out his dagger and pressed the point to Mother's breast. He poked gently, as if testing to see how much force it would take to pierce the old woman's flesh.

"We have searched through every building several times, Uncle Sarjan," said a younger man, gesturing outside. He had a thin blond moustache. "She's not here. She must have

188

left before we came, maybe as soon as the storm calmed down." He sounded almost pleading.

"Shut your mouth, Vinjan," Jai's father hissed. "She is here. I know it. There was someone inside the locked library. I want to know where she went." He turned around and pointed at his nephew with the tip of his dagger. "It is just as much in your interest to find her as it is in mine, don't you see? With this shame to our name no one will ever be willing to give you their daughter to marry. You will not find any work and you will become the laughing stock of every honorable man."

Vinjan backed down, but I saw a look of despair come over his face.

Sarjan turned back to Mother. "We will not leave your island until we find her. I can wait. But . . ." He pointed with his dagger to the three dice-players, "I do not think the crew can."

When Mother still did not say a word he grabbed her by her shoulders. "Blame yourself then. I truly tried to be an honorable man and protect you from these beasts. They are hired help, you understand. Petty criminals, jobless sailors, men on the run from the law. They want reward for their trouble. They are tired of waiting now."

Sarjan stepped back and nodded to his men. "Go ahead. Do what you like. But wait until we are outside. I do not want to hear." He signaled to his brother and nephew to follow him down the steps. Vinjan walked very fast with his head hung low.

The door closed behind them, but the men still did not move. They eyed the sisters and novices suspiciously. They fingered their weapons. They were still afraid. Sailors know that lulls and storms like they experienced at the island do not simply come out of nowhere.

But Cissil was standing there with her shiny copper hair and smooth white skin. One man grabbed hold of his knife with one hand and her arm with the other. She struggled, but nothing else happened. The man smiled broadly.

"Help yourselves!"

The other two came down the steps at once and into the cluster of women, choosing their prey. There was a quarrel at the door about which guard had to stay at his post. They still did not entirely trust that the Abbey's women would not fight back.

I saw some of them spit on the floor and touch the edges of their blades, as if to protect themselves from evil spells.

Cissil screamed. Somebody rushed forward and grabbed her other arm. It was Joem.

"No!" she cried, and I could hear her voice very clearly. "No, not her!"

I knew that she would reveal where Jai was hiding. I wanted to scream, rush forward and stop her. My heart was beating so fast my head was swimming. Joem stood in front of Cissil. I could not see Joem's face, but she stretched out her arms and hid Cissil from view.

"Take me," said Joem.

The man laughed vulgarly.

"You? Instead of the redhead? Don't be a fool." He tried to push Joem aside but she did not budge. Instead she kicked him hard in the most vulnerable place for a man. He doubled over in pain, but not for long. The next moment his fist flew through the air and met Joem's face with a terrible smacking sound. She collapsed by his feet. He grabbed Cissil by the hair with one hand and raised his knife with the other. Around the Temple more exposed daggers gleamed. This was not the resistance the men feared. There were no magic winds or inexplicable storms. This was resistance they understood, even welcomed. They had the scent of blood in their nostrils.

"Wait!" cried a voice. It was soft but still cut through all the noise.

The Rose ran up to the platform. She took off her nightgown and stood there completely naked, bathing in the first blood-red rays of the morning, which streamed in through the mosaic windows. Her hair tumbled down her back in shining curls, her breasts were full and her soft skin shimmered. She was so beautiful that nobody in the Temple could take their eyes off her. I saw what the men could not see: she was no longer servant to the Rose. She was the Goddess herself, the one who knows all the secrets of women's bodies, and all who saw her were under the enchantment of her radiant beauty.

"I am the priestess of this Temple. Servant to the Maiden.

Do you even know what that means?" She opened her arms and her smile was so beautifully compelling and powerful it hurt my eyes. "You will not have to fight with me, I will not resist. No risk of scratch marks. No tears or struggle. And I know what I am doing. I can give you pleasure beyond your wildest dreams." The Rose's voice was no longer her own, it was deep and resonant and I recognized something of the Crone's tones. The Maiden and the Crone; the beginning and the end. She pointed at the man who was still holding Cissil in a strong grip. "You are first. Follow me."

There was no chance that he would not obey. When she turned around and went through the rosewood door, the man followed her buttocks with his eyes. He let go of Cissil and bounded toward her.

"Borte, guard the door. I don't want to be disturbed." His voice sounded drunk on the beauty of the Goddess. "You'll get your turn next. Be patient. Someone has to keep an eye on the rabble here. They're not to be trusted."

"She's the most gorgeous thing I've ever seen," muttered Borte and crossed his arms. "Make sure you don't ruin her for the rest of us."

The door closed behind him.

Noises came from the altar room. Noises I did not want to hear.

Mother raised her arms. "The song of the Rose! Sing!"

She began to sing. All of the other women and girls joined in, singing in praise of the Maiden and the Rose and her wisdom and beauty, and though the men tried to stop them, they had no power against the women's song.

C rouched in the window niche, I buried my face in my hands. I did not need to look inside to know what was happening. The song said it all. Morning had come and it was time to go back to Jai and the little girls as I had promised. But I could not bring myself to leave the Temple while the men were going into the altar room one after another. I heard the Temple's main door open and shut several times. The men who were standing guard out in the yard were taking their turn too. Leaving would be like betraying the Rose.

By the time the singing stopped it was already mid-morning. I sat up and cupped my hands to peer through the window. The man who was missing some fingers, the one who had thrown stones at Bird, was sitting on the marble steps and looking at his dagger. The blade was no longer clean. The edge was matted with something dark. The fingerless man did not polish the blade, he just studied it, intently and contentedly. This was a man who liked the sight of blood.

No sounds came from the altar room. The Temple was quiet again. I had to get back to Jai. I got up and turned to leave, but a loud crash made me turn around again.

Sarjan stood in the door. Okret and Vinjan stood behind him.

"My patience has run out," he said completely calmly. "Woman, come here."

Mother walked over to him. Sarjan stepped into the Temple followed by even more of the hired crew. There were about fifteen men in total in the Temple now.

I could see Mother standing in profile, the morning light from the door falling on her sturdy figure and silver hair. The sunlight showed everything in sharp detail. Sarjan drew his dagger and held it out. It glinted in the sun as he turned it over and studied it awhile. When he spoke it was not to Mother, but to the blade itself.

"We have searched through every house on this damned island. We even discovered the other abbey in the valley, but all we found there were two scared old women. My daughter is nowhere to be found." Sarjan wiped an invisible fleck from the dagger with his sleeve and then stuck it in his belt. He nudged the fingerless man, who was now standing by Mother, the stained dagger in his hand.

"Give me your dagger." The fingerless man hesitated a moment before handing over his weapon. "The men have had a little reward but they will not stay calm for long, as you well know." He turned to Mother and raised the dagger to her chin. "So I am asking one last time—where is the harlot? Where is my ungrateful daughter who ran away from home and brought shame and dishonor to our whole family?"

"You have no daughter here," answered Mother and raised her chin as if to meet the knife's tip.

Sarjan shook his head. "See now, that was not the answer I wanted to hear. But I know that the answer is somewhere inside that hag mouth of yours." He grabbed Mother's chin and pried open her jaws. "I only have to dig it out." He stuck the saw-toothed dagger into her mouth and made a small movement.

A thin trickle of blood ran out of the corner of her mouth and down her chin. I put my hand over my mouth to keep from screaming. Mother stood completely still.

"I only have to find it," said Sarjan thoughtfully. "Where is that answer I want?" He moved the dagger again and another trickle of blood ran down the other corner of her mouth. He removed the blade and looked contentedly at its bloody edge before letting go of Mother's chin. "Well?"

"The First Mother is keeping her hidden and protected." Mother's words were muffled, and she had to swallow several times, but her voice did not falter. She was telling him the truth, but it was a truth he could not understand. She stretched out her hands to the men behind Sarjan. They stood in a tight huddle with expressionless faces.

"Hear my words," said Mother to them. "As long as you stay on this island you are in great danger. Do you not remember the storm? And the calm that came before? Go now, at once, and you will live." Blood and saliva streamed down her chin as she spoke.

Sarjan swore and smacked her in the mouth. Some of the other men were shuffling their feet nervously.

"We've been here long enough," mumbled the fingerless man. "We want our pay and to sail home now."

Sarjan turned around and threw his arms out in a

dismissive gesture. "Did I not say that you could plunder whatever you wanted?"

"But there's hardly anything worth taking," grumbled the irritated fingerless man. "Apart from a few bits of silver and gold in this temple all we've found is bed sheets and books and food and some animals. You said there'd be masses of silver!"

Sarjan grabbed him by the shoulder. "You knew the deal. It is not my fault if there is nothing here."

A discontented murmur rippled amongst the men. They scraped their feet on the floor and clenched their tattooed fists. Their brows darkened as they sank their chins angrily toward the floor. Suddenly I came to the same realization as Sarjan: he and his family, with their fine clothes and expensive weapons, were only three, while the hired men, with plain weapons and battle scars, outnumbered them by far. Mother was turning them against him. And there was only one thing that could turn them back.

He held his dagger with both hands.

"You have spread enough poison," he said, but this time his calm tone was forced. His forehead was shiny with sweat.

He raised the dagger and aimed it straight at Mother's heart with trembling hands. Mother raised her chin and met his gaze. It was clear that he was afraid of killing. Afraid of killing someone who looked him straight in the eye. But he had killed before.

Behind Mother I saw a door appear before my eyes. The tall, narrow silver door of the Crone.

I screamed but nobody noticed because at the same moment came the sound of another voice. A figure in white was standing in the doorway of the Temple, the light behind her illuminating her fair hair like an effulgence of glittering stars.

"Here I am, Father."

All eyes turned to her. Mother took a step forward and raised her hands.

"Jai, no!" she cried, and there was fear in her voice for the first time.

Jai did not look at her. She looked straight at her father as if no one else existed.

Sarjan turned his dagger to Jai. "You whore."

Jai stood there and said nothing.

Sarjan handed the bloodstained dagger back to the fingerless man. "I am putting her on the ship. Take whatever you want. We sail at midday. Okret, Vinjan, keep an eye on these others."

He grabbed Jai roughly by the arm and pushed her out into the yard.

The fingerless man, who must have been the captain of the ship, looked around. "You heard him. If it's not bolted down, take it. It doesn't look like we're getting paid any other way." Sarjan's brother Okret mumbled something, but the fingerless man ignored him.

I did not see anything else after that. I jumped down from the niche and ran. They were on their way to the goat door and I had to get there in time. I did not know what I could do to help but I did not have time to think; I had already wasted too much time, it was my fault Jai had left the crypt. I came around the side of the Temple of the Rose, leapt onto the roof of Novice House, crawled along the low roof ridge, and slid down the other side. It was a long drop down to the central courtyard but I did not stop, did not let myself hesitate. As I hit the stone paving of the yard the impact knocked the wind out of me. I rolled over and lay still for a while, gasping for air.

Maresi, whispered the Crone from the shadows. *Maresi.*

Her voice roused me to my feet. I had to catch up before it was too late. My legs could still just about carry me, so I ran. Up Dawn Steps. Nobody there. The goat door was open. I rushed through it.

They were walking along the path only a few yards ahead of me, close to the wall that reaches hip-height and protects people from falling down the steep cliff face. Jai was in front of her father. Her bare back made her look so vulnerable: a defenseless girl. I heard him talk in an uninterrupted stream that reached me as disconnected words between my own panting breaths and heavy heartbeats.

Shame. Defy me. Did you honestly believe. Like your sister. Whore. Unai.

Jai stopped in her tracks. He raised his hand and smacked the back of her head hard.

I screamed.

Sarjan spun around. Jai was behind him. One quick

movement, arms strong from Abbey work. A single push. Well aimed. The look of shock on Sarjan's face as he toppled over the wall, just where it had been destroyed by falling stones in the storm we summoned. I leaned forward and watched him fall. He bumped against the cliff face, once, twice, three times. His body landed on the rocks below but I could barely see him. Only a little bit of shiny black fabric.

Jai did not look down. She stared at her hands in awe. Then with growing realization. She stretched them out in front of her, holding them as far away from her body as she could. I wanted to run to comfort her, but just then someone rushed past and shoved me aside. It was Vinjan. He leaned over the wall and saw his uncle. He looked at Jai. She met his gaze with eyes wide and hands still outstretched in front of her.

Vinjan did not move. Neither of them cared that I was there. I prepared myself to attack him from behind if he tried to harm Jai.

"I will take my father with me," he said slowly. "I will say it was a fight. That you fell from the cliff. Both of you."

Jai said nothing.

"My father wants to leave this place. He won't climb down to look."

"Is my mother alive?"

Only at this point did her hands start trembling.

"Yes," Vinjan nodded. "He wanted . . . he wanted her to watch . . . when he punished you."

Jai lowered her hands and a smile spread over her face and transformed her completely. I barely recognized her. Her eyes were wild with happiness. "So now she is free. She is finally free!"

"I will help her, if I can."

"Tell her that I am doing well. That I have found my place. Do you promise?"

Vinjan nodded again.

"Why?" With wild eyes she urged him to answer. "Why don't you capture me? You have a weapon." She pointed at his dagger. "Why are you helping me?"

Vinjan's shoulders tensed. His voice was so quiet I could barely hear his answer.

"I have a secret. My father would kill me if he knew. The

whole time here on this island I have been thinking: next time they might come after me."

"We guessed your secret," answered Jai. He jolted in alarm and she shook her head. "Don't worry, only the women guessed. And we never said anything. You never looked at a woman the way the other men do. We noticed." The great joy had disappeared from her face and her expression was heavy-hearted. "It would probably be best for you to leave home as well. Leave our land. Find a safer place."

Then a triumphant shout came from the Abbey.

"We've found where they keep their treasure! There is a secret door in the house with all the books. Hurry, we need light!"

The crypt. They had found the crypt.

I ran without looking back to see if anybody was following me. I ran mindlessly down the mountainside sending pebbles and stones flying. I was as loud as a herd of galloping horses but I did not care. I had left them. Jai had left them. The junior novices were alone at the mercy of the men.

It is hard to explain what happened next. My memories

are blurred and what I do remember is difficult to put into words. I will do my best. Sister O said that I cannot do any more than that. Even now as I write, my hand trembles in memory of the terror, and I hope my words are still legible.

I found the hole in the mountainside and saw that Jai had got out by building up a pile of rotten boards. When I climbed down I was surrounded by total darkness and the Crone's whispers were all around me.

Maresi. Give me what is mine.

With one hand against the rock wall I started running, then fell down, then got up and carried on. My bare feet were scraping against stones and sharp edges. I could hear male voices murmuring in the distance, but they seemed impossible to reach. The passage went on and on as my breaths echoed in the darkness. I could not hear the girls.

Finally I reached the wooden door. Candlelight was flickering on the other side. I stopped. I leaned my shaking body against the rotten boards and tried to catch my breath. I was so afraid of what I might see.

I could see the oil lamp I had left with the junior novices. It had gone out. There were no little girls sleeping around it.

I could not see them anywhere. The crypt was full of men. It looked as though the whole ship's crew were gathered there. Many of them were carrying torches and lamps. They were all moving around, the reflections of flickering flames dancing on their daggers and knives. Tattooed hands scrabbled through the bones of the dead, looking for silver, looking for gold. Only one man was standing still in the middle of them all: the fingerless captain. His shaven head was turning this way and that, following the men's every movement. He snorted angrily with flared nostrils. Like an animal sniffing out the blood of its prey. One hand rested on the long saw-toothed dagger in his belt. I could not take my eyes off the blade's edge. It was now dark with blood. The Rose's blood. Mother's blood.

Maresi, whispered the Crone.

"There's no treasure here," said the fingerless man, and spat on the floor, on the crypt's sacred floor. "Only graves! Why did you bring us down here for nothing but bones?"

A short, stocky man with two daggers in his belt stopped rooting around an alcove and crossed his arms. "All folk make offerings to their dead! How was I to know that this lot don't?"

The fingerless man ran his hand over his shaven scalp and swiveled his head one more time, running his tongue back and forth over his teeth behind closed lips. The torchlight illuminated his fair beard. He froze, then grabbed a torch from the nearest man and raised it, lighting up one of the alcoves. The corner of his mouth curled up into a grotesque smile. "We might have found a little treasure after all," he said quietly. He stuck his long dagger into the opening.

"Go away!!" shouted a little voice. Heo.

There was no screaming or crying. Only that short command: Go away! My brave little ones. They were all alone when they had heard the men come. They had done the only thing they could do, which was to find a hiding place. If I had been there I could have led them out. Now they were stuck like mice in a trap. Standing pressed against the door, I could see everything clearly, despite the smoke from the torches and lamps, but I could not bring myself to move. It was all my fault. I had failed in the only thing Mother had asked me to do. My heart slowed down, as if it wanted to stop beating completely out of shame and fear.

"We can sell these young ones for a good price. It's

easy to prepare them for the whorehouses. I know many a merchant who would gladly buy the whole lot." The fingerless man smacked his lips and poked his dagger into the alcove. "I can begin teaching them myself, on the sail home. Girls this young are so much more submissive. More tender."

"Go away!" said Heo again. "The Goddess will punish you. Can't you feel that she is already here?"

The men laughed. But I could feel it. The Crone was breathing so heavily from the alcoves and the corners it was hard to believe the men could not hear her. *Maresi*, she whispered. *My hunger.* I pressed my hands over my mouth to stop myself from screaming.

The fingerless man handed his torch over, stuck a hand into the alcove, and dragged Heo out. He pulled her up onto her feet in front of him, holding her skinny little arms in a tight grasp. I saw her slender neck and bare little feet. I saw his heavy hand press between her legs.

Then I forced myself to move. By Goddess, it was difficult. I was so terrified. My shame in writing this now is just as great as my terror was then. Shame that I could not even rush forward to help Heo when I saw that she was in danger. It was a painstaking process as I slowly forced myself to crawl through the hole in the door. My legs could barely hold me up. I was still pressing my hand over my mouth. Heo was screaming now, but I was still walking as though through thick clay. I was so scared of the men's sharp weapons. They caught sight of me, pointed their weapons at me, opened their dark mouths, and bellowed. Then I saw it: the Crone's silver door. It appeared in the stone wall to my right as if it had always been there. As vivid and real as any other door on the island. Worn around the edges. A handle polished by time. A door that divided the world into inside and outside, like all doors. Still closed, still separating our world from the realm and the hunger of the Crone.

Maresi, whispered the Crone as I walked toward the fingerless man. *Maresi*, she called as he pushed Heo aside and plunged the dagger into my belly. As my blood ran down the blade, it mixed with the blood of the Rose and Mother: the first and second aspects of the Goddess. They were the beginning and I was the end. The Crone's voice grew stronger. It filled me until I barely heard Heo's screams. I collapsed and landed in the Crone's shadows. While I crawled toward the door she whispered and told me her true name. I slipped and I slithered along the wet stone floor. My hands were red with my own blood. The Crone's shadows were caressing me, pulling me in. I stretched toward the door handle but could not reach it. I had to get up. I leaned against the wall with one hand pressed over my wound. *Give me what belongs to me,* hissed the Goddess of darkness and pain, and I obeyed her and opened her door.

The darkness on the other side was blacker than anything in this world, so black it blinded me. I fell to my knees with my mouth full of blood, unable to see. But I could hear.

The Crone extended her power through the door and accepted the sacrifice of those who had wandered into her crypt. One by one they hit the stone floor like rag dolls, and I heard cries, screams, and the cracking of bones. They screamed in horror as soon as they realized they were facing their own deaths. Their terror filled the whole crypt. The air soured with the smell of intestines and feces. Torches hissed as they were extinguished on the wet, bloody floor. The Crone crushed them like the vermin they were.

My own blood was flowing between my fingers and

down on the ground in front of the door, and I knew it was my blood that was holding it open. I fought against unconsciousness and the terrible pain that was threatening to drag me down into the darkness. I had to do this final thing for my little sisters. For the Crone.

The Crone opened her jaws and I could feel her sour breath on my cheek. She took a deep breath and sucked the men to her, one after another. They screamed as they smacked down on the stone floor, still alive. She wanted them alive and whole, she wanted their bodies and souls. She wanted no remains left to bury. Complete obliteration. I could smell them, the smell of sweat and steel and blood. Some reached for me as they tried to stop their mutilated bodies from being sucked through the door, but the men's fingers were nothing against the power of the Crone. Once they were through the door and confronted with the silence inside, their screams were cut off abruptly.

When it was completely quiet in the crypt I finally let myself collapse to the floor. Now it was done. Now it was only me and the Crone. Now it was my turn.

Maresi. You belong to me. Can you see that now?

I could not answer. My voice was gone. I lay on the threshold to her realm and knew that what she said was true. That is why I had never been called to any house. She had already marked me and chosen me in the hunger winter. I was hers.

Come to me and you will not suffer anymore, she said in a tender, maternal tone. For the Crone and the Mother and the Maiden are one, they are only different aspects of the Goddess. *Come here where everything begins and ends, where everything dies and is born anew. You value knowledge more than anything. The ultimate knowledge is here. Everything you have ever wished for. Come to me.*

I knew that she had the power to force me. But she was not forcing, she was asking.

Someone grabbed my hand, and I clung to it hard as the darkness fell.

Sometimes I think I chose the cowardly way out. The right thing to do, the braver thing, would have been to go through the door and see what was on the other side. The Crone was offering me knowledge beyond my wildest dreams. Knowledge I will never have in this world. I am curious. More than curious: sometimes it keeps me awake at night and I physically ache with yearning. But I did not have the courage. I want to stay here in this world as long as I possibly can. I want to live amongst books and goats and wind and nadum bread. I want to grow up to see what the world has to offer me and what I have to offer the world. I am not finished with it, not yet.

The first thing I saw when I woke up was Jai. Her pale face framed by golden hair. The rings under her eyes were darker than ever before, and darkness still inhabited my vision, which made it difficult to see. My body felt lifeless, as though it were still sleeping while my mind was awake. I tried to speak but my tongue was too dry.

"Praise Mother," whispered Jai. "You are still with us. Here, wet your lips, but you mustn't drink anything yet."

She held a cup of cool water to my mouth. It was difficult to resist gulping it all down immediately, but I wet my lips and tongue and enjoyed the slight relief it afforded me.

"I will get Sister Nar," she said and got up.

"Wait." My voice was so weak I could hardly hear myself, but Jai stopped. "First tell me what happened."

Jai smiled one of her rare smiles. "Now I know you are on the mend. You are already asking questions." She adjusted my blanket, but I felt so detached from my body I could barely sense where it lay over my chest. Jai saw the worry in my eyes and her smile disappeared.

"Sister Nar has given you strong herbs to lessen the pain while your body heals itself. It is a serious, deep wound you have got in your belly. You have had a fever." She fiddled with something on the table next to my bed. "We have been . . . We thought you would leave us."

I wanted to ask how long I had been lying there, but it was too many words to get out. Jai saw the question in my eyes anyway.

"You have been here in Sister Nar's room for three days. And she says you will have to stay awhile yet."

Something moved underneath my bed. A little black head popped up and squinted at me. "Maresi! You are awake!"

"Shh, not so loud. Maresi wants some answers before Sister Nar comes." Jai turned to me. "Heo has been sleeping on the floor by your bed the whole time."

"Well, I couldn't leave you," said Heo, and took hold of my hand. I winced, remembering how I had left her. Heo pulled her hand away at once.

"Did that hurt?"

I forced myself to smile. "No. Please hold. Good."

Heo smiled with relief and held my hand extremely carefully. I recognized the feeling of her fingers around mine.

"You held me," I said. My words were strained and grating. "In the crypt."

Heo nodded earnestly. "Yes. When the man stabbed you a huge darkness came. The girls hid in the alcove, and all the men screamed and screamed and it was terrible. You were lying on the floor and there was so much blood, Maresi. I was so scared. I held you because I was afraid you were going to die."

"You saved me," I said. "You kept me here."

Heo said nothing and just squeezed my hand. I think she already knew she had saved my life. I believe that girl knows more than people think, in between all her chatter.

I looked at Jai. The next question was the hardest.

"Everyone . . . is everyone . . ."

"Yes. Everyone is alive, Maresi. Including the Rose, though she has been wounded. There were three men guarding the Temple who did not go down into the crypt. When they heard the screams, and then when the other men never returned, my uncle and Vinjan soon led them back to the ship and they sailed away. I released the sisters and novices."

"Then they came down to the crypt," said Heo, "and fetched Ismi and the others. Sister Nar dressed your wounds and we carried you here."

"Heo, I am sorry. I never should have—"

"Hush, Maresi," Heo said in a strict voice, almost like

Sister O. "You did the right thing. You always did what you thought best."

"That is more than you could say about me," said Jai bitterly. "I should have given myself up straight away and none of this would have happened."

"Well, then, you'd have sailed north by now," said Heo.

I looked at Jai and she nodded. "Yes, I told them what I did. About my father's death. I could not live with such a terrible secret."

"No one blames her," said Heo emphatically. "Mother says she would have done the same if she could have."

I wanted to ask more but the medicine started to fade, and as I came back to my body I felt such indescribable pain that I could not speak. Jai went pale and ran off to get Sister Nar, who came at once with compresses and decoctions, and I sank back into a deep, dreamless sleep.

As I gradually grew stronger I started drinking water, then eating and receiving visits. First my friends came to see me: Ennike, Dori, Toulan, and Cissil. I was even happy to see Joem. They entertained me with stories and jokes, which made my scars ache when I tried not to laugh. I had time to myself as well. Time to lie in bed and think. There was a lot to think about. A decision started forming in my head, a decision I did not want to face up to. I knew the right thing to do. But I did not know if I would be brave enough to follow it through. There were many nights when I could not sleep for the pain, and I spent the time grappling with my conscience while the moon gazed at me through the window.

Sister Nar kept a watchful eye over me. At some point she must have decided that my health was returning, because I woke up one morning with Mother standing by my bed. Sister O was behind her, with a straight back and an unreadable expression on her face. I wanted her to sit on the edge of my bed and stroke my hair, but she stayed behind Mother.

"Maresi. Sister Nar says that you are feeling better," said Mother.

I tried to sit up in bed. "Yes, much better. I do not need herbs to dull the pain anymore and I can eat liquid food."

"No need to get up." She pulled a chair up to my bed and sat down. "Can you tell us what happened in the crypt?"

"The Crone was there." I stopped to think where to begin and Mother nodded encouragingly. "I saw her door during Moon Dance. She called to me. I recognized her door, I had seen it at home when my little sister died. The winter when we were all starving. I was scared. I thought she wanted to take me." I shook my head. "I misunderstood. After that I was living in fear, I heard her voice everywhere, I was scared that she would come and get me. When the men came I could sense the door again. It was here on the island, it was waiting. I thought it meant I was going to die."

I looked to Sister O, seeking comfort, but she gazed fixedly at me with tightly pressed lips. I looked away.

"When I heard the men shouting that they had found

the crypt I thought about the little girls alone in there. I ran down through the entrance that the Crone herself had shown me. Her door was there and I knew I had to open it to satisfy her hunger. She had chosen me, not to die, but to open her realm."

"Did she call to you?" asked Sister O. "Did she command you to follow the men through the door?"

I shook my head. "No. She asked me to come, but she did not command me."

Mother exchanged a glance with Sister O before turning back to me.

"Maresi. You have been in the Abbey for a long time but you do not have a house. I have wondered why nobody has called you. But now I see that you have found your calling." She leaned forward.

Here it comes, I thought. She was going to ask me to become her novice. I knew what my answer must be, but I did not know how I could say it.

"The Crone has vast knowledge," she continued. "Some of which can be seen from the outside, but there is much that is hidden too. Concealed from most people. That is why her servant also works in secret." She turned to Sister O.

Suddenly I understood. The snake on Sister O's door. Her affinity with books and knowledge, everything associated with the Crone. She met my gaze but still said nothing. Mother continued.

"Sister O is not a name. It is a title, just as the servant to the Rose is a title, passed down from sister to novice. The O is the eternal circle, the snake biting its tail." Mother drew a circle in the air with one finger and I could almost see the snake in front of me, with blank black eyes and its tail in its mouth. "Sister O serves the secrets of the Crone. Secrets that the Crone has now revealed to you."

My heart began to race.

"Maresi." Sister O's voice was rougher than ever. Deep and raspy, like the voice of the Crone. "My mistress has called you. She has not commanded, but asked. Now I will do the same. Would you like to be my novice?"

I burst into tears. I cried so hard my body convulsed, tears and snot ran down my face and I could barely breathe.

Mother was at a loss, but Sister O came straight to my side, sat on my bed, and held me and stroked my hair.

"There, there, little one. Do not worry. Tell us what is weighing on you, my Maresi."

When I could finally speak, every single word pained me even more than the wound in my belly. I clutched Sister O tight and sobbed into her breast.

"There is nothing I want more, Sister. It is like a dream I did not even dare think possible. To be your novice and learn everything you know, and stay in the treasure chamber and read as much as I want . . ." Sister O chuckled quietly and gave me a little squeeze. "But I have to say no. I . . ."

The words refused to come out. She would be angry. She would be disappointed in me. I spoke as fast as I could, pouring out all the words before I could change my mind.

"This is the dearest place to me on earth. I cannot think of anything more wonderful than spending my whole life here studying and reading and teaching. But it would not be right. Sister O, we cannot shut out the world. It affects us, even here. It would be selfish of me to stay here where

I am safe, when I could use everything you have taught me to do a lot of good. The people in my homeland are ruled by superstition and ignorance. A fraction of what I have learned here could save people dying from starvation and disease. It could change how women and men see themselves and one another; it could open up a new window to the wider world. I must go home again and see what I can do for my people."

Sister O and Mother listened to me in silence. Then Mother leaned back in her chair. "The Crone has given you great wisdom for one so young."

Sister O turned to Mother almost angrily. "But her courage is entirely her own!"

Sister O took me up to the Temple Yard yesterday morning. It was early, long before anyone was out for the sun greeting. The sun was not up yet and it smelled like the island always does on summer mornings: like rocks seeped in yesterday's warmth, wild oregano and cypress, seaweed and dew. A koan bird flew over our heads in a purposeful straight line and gave out a single short screech. We stood side by side in silence and looked out, not over the sea but over the houses and roofs of the Abbey. Smoke was coming out of the Hearth House chimney. Sister Ers wakes up early.

The sun's first rays peeked over White Lady, tinging the sky and mountaintop gold. I realized I had never greeted the sun from the Temple Yard and now I never will. I will never become a sister, never stand with all the other sisters and carry out the familiar movements. I blinked a few times and turned around. Sister O laid her veiny, sunburned hand on my shoulder and turned me back to face the sun again.

225

"Maresi," she said and her voice was sterner than usual. "Look around you. This is the other side of death. Life! And this side is even stronger." She was quiet for a moment, and we stood side by side and watched the world explode into light as the sun rose over the mountain. Sister O turned to me. "I know the sacrifice you are making. You think nobody understands, but I do."

I shook my head and she raised my chin so that I had to look her in the eyes. Her cheeks were wet with tears but her voice was steady. "It was a sacrifice I could not make, Maresi. I chose to stay here. I chose safety and books and knowledge. What the Crone had to offer me was too great a temptation. I turned my back on the world. But you have seen that it does not work, that the world finds you wherever you are and it is cowardly to try to hide. You are much wiser than I, little Maresi."

I took her hand and pressed it to my cheek. She smiled at me and wiped away her tears.

"Always thinking of others. Your path will not be easy; you worry too much about people. That is what makes you unique. I will do everything I can to provide you with as much as possible for your journey. I have spoken to Mother." Her smile grew wider. "You are too young to leave us yet. You must study more of everything before you can go back home. You may study anything you want. Sister Nar can teach you about herbs and healing, Sister Mareane about animal care, Mother herself about silver and numbers, Sister Loeni about the secrets of the Blood." She chuckled when she saw my expression. "She has much to teach, Maresi."

I did not know what to say. It is too fantastic, too incredible. I have never heard of anyone studying *everything*. It will make it so much easier for me to return and realize my dream of founding a school in my green valley.

From the central courtyard I could hear the Novice House door opening. The Abbey was coming to life and soon the sisters would stream into the Temple Yard. But Sister O still had not said the most important thing. I squeezed her fingers and my bottom lip trembled.

Then her smile suddenly softened, and she pulled me close and held me against her bony body.

"Maresi," she mumbled into my headscarf. "You will become my novice. Novice to the Knowledge. To the Crone.

As long as I can keep you here at the Abbey, you are my little girl."

I held her tight there in the Temple Yard. I am the happiest girl who ever found shelter at the Abbey. I have gained so much and I am about to gain even more.

ow I have written down everything I can remember. I have been sitting in Sister O's room for many days, writing with the same quill I have seen her use so many times. I am wearing the ring she gave me on my finger. A ring in the shape of a snake biting its own tail.

Jai and Ennike have taken it in turns to bring me food, but no one else has been allowed to disturb me. It has only been me and the light drifting through the room and the scratch of the feather pen against the coarse paper. The sounds of the Abbey float in: the laughter of the junior novices, the bleating of the goats, sandal-clad feet against the stone paving, the call of seabirds. All the sounds that should be there are there. The silence that reigned when the men came to the island is merely a memory now, a memory I hope will leave me in peace when I bind it to the page.

At night I have been sleeping dreamlessly, and I am no longer afraid of the darkness around and inside me. The Crone will not take me home. Not yet. I still fear the moment when she does, but I believe it is a fear I can get over. Sister O will help me, as will the Abbey, and all my friends here. I believe that if you live life fearlessly, with your whole heart, then in the end you cannot fear death either. They are two sides of the same thing. One day I will give myself over to the Crone, and she will reveal her mysteries to me. A small part of me thinks of that time with curiosity and maybe even anticipation. Perhaps all of me can see it that way, once the door opens again. But first I must live— live and learn and use my knowledge so the Crone can be proud of me when we meet.

I am glad that Sister O encouraged me to write down my story. The act alone has afforded me some peace: to put pen to paper, to see my experiences take on words. It feels as if the act of writing has already turned it into a new myth, a saga, one of the many stories that surround the Abbey. I also feel that I did not truly understand what happened before I wrote it down. Now I understand it a little better, but it also feels more distant. As if it happened to someone else, someone called Maresi who opened the Crone's door, and not me, the Abbey novice Maresi from Rovas. I cannot explain it any better than that.

This evening Sister O and I will put my book in the treasure chamber amongst the other important tales of the Abbey. It feels strange to think of my words next to books I have read so many times, but Sister O says that that is where it belongs. It fills me with pride. My words, Maresi's words, will live on in the Abbey library for centuries to come. These words will still be here long after I am gone. The thought makes me reel in amazement, like when I look up at a night sky strewn with stars.

So that is the story of what happened when Jai came to the Abbey in the nineteenth year of the reign of the thirty-second Mother, when the Crone spoke to me and the women combed forth a storm. That is what happened when the island of Menos sent a warning message about the presence of unknown men, when the Rose sacrificed herself for her sisters and when I, Abbey novice Maresi from Rovas, opened the door of the Crone.

I am once again writing at Sister O's desk. For the past three years it has been my desk too. The quill is the same. Am I the same? Do we change so much with the passing of time that we are not the same person from one year to the next? I have just read through what I wrote after the men came to the island, and it is strange to think that it was actually I who experienced it all. It feels so distant, and yet I know that what happened is an inextricable part of who I am now.

It is time for me to go. Even writing those words is difficult, let alone thinking about what they entail. It is not as though I am unprepared. Over the past few years the whole Abbey has been dedicated to my preparation. I have had more schooling than any other novice and studied and worked as hard as I possibly could under all the sisters. I have read the Moon House secret scrolls, which only a privileged few may study. I even spent an autumn on White Lady. I cannot divulge what happened up there, but I learned what did in fact take place when I believed that birds lifted me over the wall. Of course there is plenty still to learn, there always is, but now the time is ripe.

It was hunger that brought me to the Abbey: a lack of food. Once again I fear hunger, but this time it is a lack of knowledge that scares me. Here at the Abbey there are books. Here there are people with more to teach me. How will I satisfy my hunger without them? Mother says that there is a lot for me to learn out in the world. Things no one else can teach me and things that cannot be learned from books. I know she is right. It is hard-won knowledge. I will have to pay for it in a way that I do not yet understand. I prefer knowledge I can gather from books.

Jai has been extremely busy since becoming Sister Nummel's novice last summer. Three new junior novices came to the island last autumn and they all chose to be Jai's special little protégées. Despite this, she has spent all her free time sewing the clothes I will need when I leave: tunics and trousers and headscarves. I have decided to continue dressing like an Abbey novice and not in customary Rovas attire. I will be different and conspicuous whatever I do, and I think the Abbey attire might afford me a little security. My outfit is already folded up in a bag with sprigs of dried lavender. Jai packed it herself yesterday. She says I am far too impractical to pack.

"If it were up to you you'd only take books," she snorted and brushed off some dry lavender flowers from her clothes. She was right. Unfortunately I cannot bring many books with me. When I was alone in the dormitory again I opened the bag and was hit by the smell of linen, soap, and lavender. It smelled like home. That smell will be more precious than any books.

Jai also secretly made me a bloodsnail-red woolen cloak. Toulan dyed the yarn during the last snail harvest and Ranna and Ydda, who are skilled weavers, wove the fabric. Then Jai sewed every stitch herself and would not let anyone help her. She gave me the cloak one evening when we were sitting under the lemon tree and talking as usual. She avoided my eye as she handed it to me.

"For the cold nights in Rovas," she said simply, and stared out to sea. She has finally started to admit that snow might actually exist.

"But Jai," was all I could say. I took her hand and held it like she used to hold mine during the nights when the darkness frightened me. I knew she was thinking of them, too. I was also thinking that I will have no one to hold my hand at night from now on.

The cloak is much too valuable for someone like me, but Mother decided that I should have it. "You are still young. The cloak will give you the respect you need. No one will dare defy a woman, however young, who is dressed in a cloak like this." That is what she said yesterday when she called me to her room in Moon House for a few final words.

"Rovas is a vassal state," I answered, and fingered the cloak's silk lining, which Jai had sewn down with invisibly small stitches. "We cannot enact our own laws. We cannot educate our own children. The ruler of Urundien wants to keep us in ignorance. I do not know how I will go about setting up my school."

Mother raised her eyebrows.

"Did you think your mission would be easy?" She looked at me sternly. "Maresi. You must find your own way now. But I have every faith in you." Then she smiled one of her rare, roguish smiles, which made her look like a young novice. "Heo, fetch my purse."

Heo grinned proudly at me and unlocked one of the near-invisible doors behind Mother's writing desk. These are doors that conceal secrets. Heo is Mother's novice now. The youngest novice ever called to Moon House. How did we not see it all along? Heo was the obvious choice for Moon House! We were fooled by her playfulness and her incorrigible joy. But behind that she has enormous integrity. She is totally and utterly herself. It is no coincidence that she was the one who held me on this side of the Crone's door.

Heo brought out a fat leather purse and handed it to Mother, who weighed it in her hand before holding it out to me.

"This will open many doors for you that would otherwise be closed."

I opened the purse. It was filled with shiny silver coins; not a single copper. After studying with Mother for several moons I knew that this was as much as the Abbey's whole annual income. "Mother. This is too much."

Mother snorted. "It will not last long. When the silver has run out you will have nothing more than your keen wits to live on. And this." She held out her hand and Heo placed something in it. It was a large comb of shining copper. "The Rose requested I give you this as a farewell present. She has polished it herself."

Ennike is the servant to the Rose now. I am supposed to stop calling her Ennike, but Jai and I have difficulty remembering her new title. Eostre, who was the Rose before Ennike, always corrects us strictly. "How can she fulfill her role if you insist on reminding her of the past!" she says. We always nod solemnly and agree, but as soon as she looks the other way we make funny faces at her baby daughter Geja until she chokes with laughter. She is a happy, chubby little girl. Strong. When I look at her I think of Anner and how weak she was. If we had known better, if we had known about nutrition and healing, we could have given her a better start in life. Then maybe she could have made it through the hunger winter. This is one of the reasons I feel I must go home. The knowledge I have gained at the Abbey can save lives.

Eostre could not continue as servant to the Rose after she had Geja. This is not on account of the scars from the fingerless man's knife. Eostre herself has said that she is happy he cut her. It was thanks to him that her blood was on the dagger and mixed with Mother's and mine, so that the Crone's door could be opened. The fingerless man had not cut deep; his objective was not to kill but to inflict pain. To disfigure. Eostre is still beautiful; no scars in the world can cover that. Geja is what changed everything. Eostre is now taking part in another of the First Mother's mysteries. One day she will become servant to Havva, I believe. Those who have had a child of their own are close to Havva. Geja just has to grow a little bigger first. Right now Eostre is Geja's mother and nothing else, and it suits her well. She looks happy. Happy and tired.

I looked at the comb in Mother's hand. I thought about how much Ennike must have polished it to get it so gleaming. I thought about how I was her shadow when I first came here, how she was my first friend. Would I ever see her again? Would I ever see anyone from the Abbey again?

"The comb is the Abbey's protection," I said slowly. "You need it."

"Stop protesting against all the gifts," said Heo and furrowed her brow. "We want to give them to you. You need protection too. You and all the new pupils you will have and love." She tightened her fists.

I walked around Mother's writing desk and laid my arms around Heo. She stood stiff and unhappy, but she let me hug her. "Not as much as I love you, I hope you know that." I whispered in her hair. It smelled like sun and sea and Heo. "I will write often. As soon as I find someone who can take the letters south. Do you promise you will write to me?"

"*Must* you go, Maresi?" asked Heo. Her body went soft and she wrapped her arms hard around my middle. "I am going to miss you so much. I miss you already." She dried her runny nose on my tunic.

I had to swallow several times before I could answer. There was so much I wanted to say.

"I will miss you too. So much. But I must."

I held her for a long time. All too short a time. Mother looked at me over Heo's head.

"Do not be sad, Maresi. You have to let go of the old to begin something new. But that does not mean it is lost forever."

A spark of hope ignited in me. Mother sees things in her trances: things about the future. I opened my mouth to speak but Mother shook her head. "It is never good to know too much about what is going to happen. Your own future is not a gift I can give you. We have given you what we can. Now the rest is up to you."

ω

Now the rest is up to me. I have never been so afraid. Not even in the crypt, at the Crone's door.

A Vallerian fishing boat is coming to take me tomorrow at dawn. I must sail with it to Muerio, the town where I first saw the sea. Then I will leave the sea behind and continue northward over land. Mother has arranged my transport for the first leg and from there I can find my own way. All the sisters and novices have promised to sing me off. They will stand in the Abbey's yards and dress the stairs as I step aboard, and their song will gently sway me out to sea. It will be like Moon Dance, but this time I cannot turn around in the middle of the labyrinth and return to them. This time I must keep going forward until I can no longer see or hear my friends. My family.

This final evening I will let the ink dry on my words and then put my book back in the treasure chamber. Yes, I still call it that. Not even Sister Loeni's seriousness has been able to dispel my childish wonder at the treasures contained in all the Abbey's books. Soon I will tear Ennike, I mean the Rose, away from her duties, and help Jai shirk the tasks given to her by Sister Nummel, and then the three of us will sit together in Knowledge Garden and talk one last time. They will always be my sisters, though I will never become a sister here myself. I do not know how I will cope in the outside world without their laughter and friendship. But so it must be.

ᚹ

A farewell feast will be held in Hearth House tonight. All the sisters and novices are coming, and I can already smell the tempting aroma of nadum bread. Eostre has promised me that Geja will be with us for as long as she stays awake. Geja's blond hair and curious eyes will be the image I carry with me as a reminder that life goes on. Whatever happens, life finds a way forward.

It is going to be a party to remember. I can hardly believe it is being held in my honor, when only seven years ago I came here as a little girl who licked doors and did not know how to behave herself. After the meal I will go down to the crypt and make an offering to the Crone and bestow my thanks on the bones of the First Sisters.

Then, last of all, Sister O and I will sit together in the Temple Yard and watch the sun set over the sea.